Sage

SARAH LAMB

A thank you to my proofreader, Brooke, and all of the lovely women who help ARC read to catch those typos I miss!

Paperback ISBN: 978-1-960418-66-1

Contents

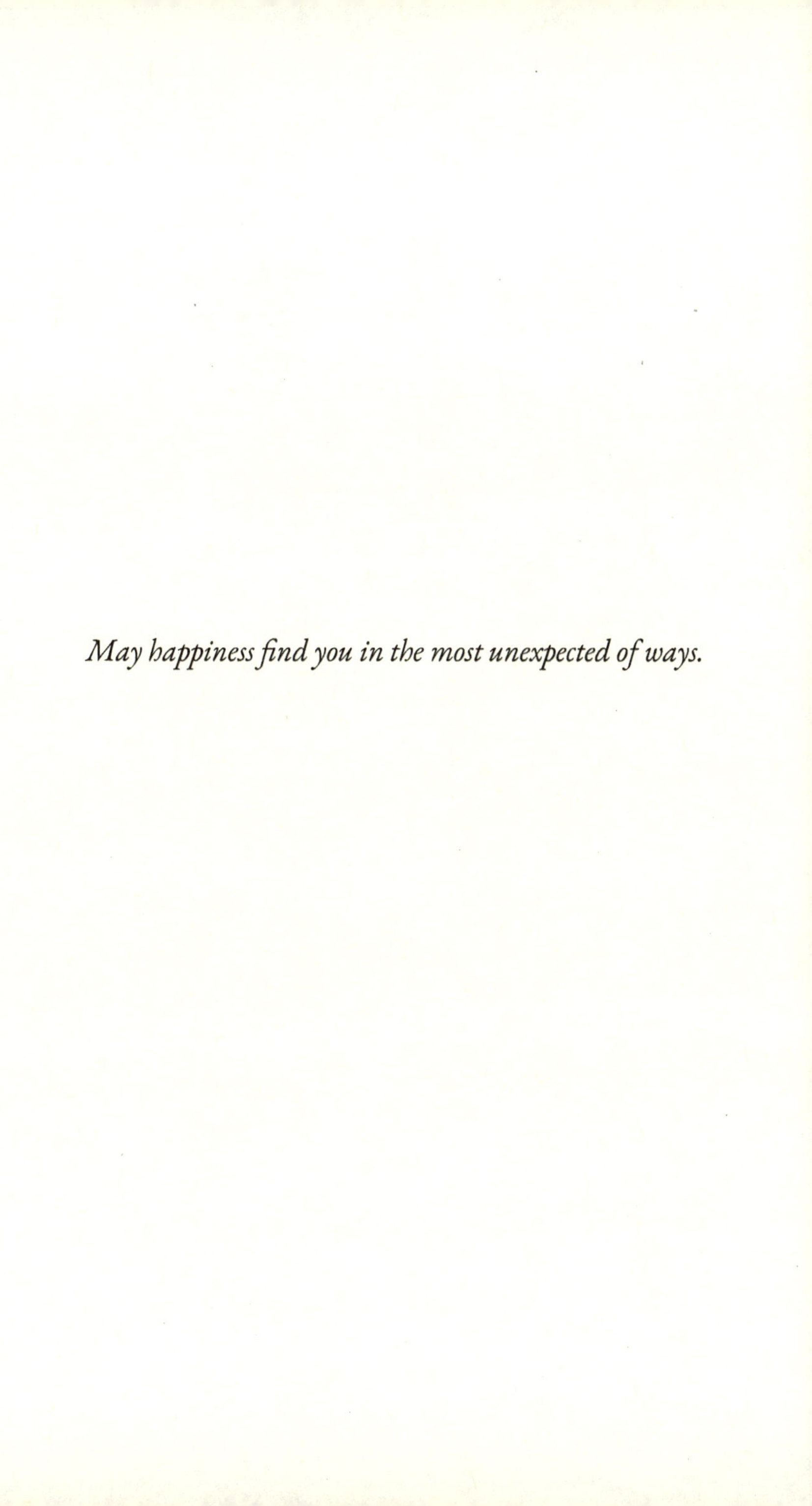

May happiness find you in the most unexpected of ways.

Welcome to Garden Belles Mail-Order Brides

Established in 1850, during the height of the westward wagon train exodus, and the various land runs. Men, desperate for a partner, a wife, turned to Saint Louis sisters Dahlia and Zinnia Williams (aka the Garden Belles) for assistance.

The sisters, both spinsters, are especially proud of three things in the lives: their garden, filled with every type of imaginable flower; their penchant for finding perfect wives for most suitable husbands; and more importantly, the orphaned niece they raised from a baby.

Join us as more would-be brides are matched with eager husbands for their own happily-ever-afters.

The Garden Belles are retiring and you're invited to the party! Enjoy yourself with this year's final three books!

Chapter 1

Zinnia watched the rain stream down the glass windowpane. "It feels like it's been raining for days," she said with a frown. "I hope we don't get fungus specks on the roses now."

"I don't even want to think about what it will do to the irises," her sister, Dahlia, sighed. "Or the poppies we just planted. The whole garden will be a mess from this storm. It will take days to clean it up again. Do you see all the debris the wind has blown in?"

At that very moment, there was a crack of thunder, and a branch broke off one of the trees in the garden, skittering across and landing in the ferns.

"Thank goodness that wasn't any larger," Zinnia said. "I don't think anything is damaged. But, I can't watch any longer. My nerves can't handle it. I simply must take my mind off the storm and what it's doing to our lovely garden. Should we get to work?"

"The tea is made, there are slices of cinnamon cake at the ready, and I've the letters sorted by male and female," Dahlia said, leading the way to the cozy kitchen table.

"Good. Let's start. There's been one on my mind ever since we got it," Zinnia said. "I'm concerned, though, that we don't have the person she needs."

"Sage." Dahlia sat heavily, and shook her head. "The poor girl."

"Maybe there's someone in today's letters," Zinnia said, reaching for the newest arrivals. "Only two? Well, we will hope for the best."

She handed her sister one envelope, and set to work peeling open the one she had.

"No good," Dahlia said. "This is from a woman. I think she will be quite easy to place though. She says she is willing to go anyplace and wed anyone. What of yours? Could it be for Sage, I mean."

"Mine might work," Zinnia said, though her voice was hesitant. "It is for a man. However, it was written by his mother."

"Oh? Sometimes those are the best," Dahlia said. "Of course, they can also be the worst."

"Well, she describes her son as intelligent, handsome, and hardworking."

"What mother wouldn't?" Dahlia said. "What else does she say?"

Zinnia set the letter between them and pointed. "That he must get married, and quickly, and he's been reluctant to do so. She doesn't say why, nor why the urgency, only that it's of great importance. His mother says her son can easily provide, and would do best with a young woman who is of some intellect and enjoys reading. She's sent money for travel expenses."

She held it up, and both stared at the vast amount.

"There's enough for two to travel comfortably," Dahlia said quietly, meeting her sister's eyes.

"But are they suited?" Zinnia asked. "Also, with so little to go on, how might he feel, her housekeeper arriving with her?"

"Her chaperone," Dahlia corrected. "If it doesn't work out, then she's not alone. And perhaps she can find someone else."

"You are right," Zinnia agreed. She pinched the bridge of her nose. "There's nothing else for her, and I know how little time she has left. Though there are few details on the man, my instincts tell me he is her best chance."

"I agree." Dahlia sighed. "I don't like it myself, but sometimes all we can do is hope for the best."

"Well then, shall we write Miss Robinson, and tell her there is a Mr. Walker waiting to make her acquaintance?" her sister asked.

"Why be so formal sounding? We always use their first names when we send out letters," Dahlia protested.

"Yes, but if he's worth a good deal of money, as this letter from his mother and the sum enclosed leads me to believe, perhaps he'll expect an introduction such as that. At the very least, his mother will." Zinnia crossed her arms, and raised her brows. "Isn't that how it's done in the upper class? All miss and mister?"

"You are right," Dahlia said. "We wouldn't want to mess that up! Well then, I'll write her letter, and you write his."

Quietly, they penned the letters, hoping that this wouldn't be the time they made a mistake. That this young woman, so desperately in need, would find her happy ending with the young man who, actually, didn't want a wife at all.

Chapter 2

Though it was incredibly stifling and humid in the house, Sage wouldn't dream of complaining. The previous winter, when they had almost no fuel at all for the fire and had worn every possible layer on their bodies to shiver less, Sage had longed for these warm, even hot days.

Of course, being warm enough wouldn't be a problem this winter. In four days, the house would be taken by the man her brother had sold it to, and she and Mrs. Erics would be homeless.

Sage bit her lip and glanced over at her housekeeper and friend. Mrs. Erics was dropping some dandelion greens and sliced tubers and wild mushrooms she'd collected into a pot that was more water than broth, but it didn't matter. It would fill their bellies, at least for another meal. Perhaps she'd plead full, and there would be enough for tomorrow.

Especially if she could find something more to add to it. Could one eat bark, if it was boiled? She tried to recall if she'd ever read about that.

"I am failing at my job," the housekeeper said, as though sensing Sage's eyes on her or her thoughts about the scanty meal.

"Nonsense," Sage answered lightly. "You could never. There's not a person kinder, nor more resourceful and hardworking. Do you know how much I adore you?"

"I'm to take care of you," Mrs. Erics said firmly, gripping the cooking spoon firmer. "Your father said so. From the moment you came into this world, you were in my care. I promised your mother I would always look after you as she took her final breaths after your birth."

"And no one could have done a better job," Sage told her. "You have been every bit a mother to me, as kind and as loving. It amazes me to think that we have known each other for twenty-three years. And," she added, putting her hands on her friend's shoulders, "you've done a wonderful job. It is I who have failed. Losing my job? If I had that, we could have found a room to live in somewhere."

"You didn't lose it. They let you go because they couldn't afford to pay you," Mrs. Erics reminded her.

While that was true, it didn't make her feel much better. Sage hesitated. "You...you don't have to stay, you know. This last year, when we've had nothing... I feel terrible.

When was the last time you were paid? Forget that! When was the last time you were fed properly?"

"That's not important," Mrs. Erics said, jutting her chin out. "Staying with you is. You're every bit my own child."

A lump formed in her throat. Sage couldn't imagine being away from Mrs. Erics. If only she had a way to provide for the woman who took such good care of her. Her eyes fell on the soup again that Mrs. Erics was stirring, as though it would thicken by her ministrations.

"I will miss my job," Sage sighed. "Not that the bakery paid much for all of the hard work it required, but getting to have the leftover rolls each day was helpful."

"Who needs them? I'm tired of rolls," Mrs. Erics said, waving her hand about.

"So am I," Sage answered with a smile, though she knew they were both lying. Without her job, the luxury of more than watery soup from foraged plants wouldn't exist. And what would happen this winter, when snow covered the forest floor?

Perhaps more pressing was what would happen in those quickly approaching days, when she and Mrs. Erics were alone without any shelter over their heads, and no income to provide any. Could one live in the woods? Perhaps in the summer, but there was no doubt it would be impossible in the winter.

"Didn't you say you got a letter?" Mrs. Erics asked suddenly, pulling Sage from her thoughts.

"Yes. From Jerry." Sage pulled the letter from her brother out of her dress pocket. "I'm not sure I want to open it. I'm still very upset at him. What did he think would happen, him selling the house? He knew we'd never be able to support ourselves."

"You must read it," her friend said. "Perhaps it's something that can help."

"Knowing Jerry, it won't be," Sage said, holding the envelope with two hands, and not even letting herself hope that it would contain even a measure of good news.

She couldn't help the small frown as she thought about her older brother. When he'd left to marry a woman named Lorelei three years ago, he'd also left Sage and Mrs. Erics with only a few hundred dollars and a number of false promises.

He promised to keep providing. He promised to write often. He promised to send for them, if they needed to leave. Though he wrote on occasion, he'd done nothing more to help them, though he knew how much of a struggle it had been. Though Sage wouldn't let on to others, she made plain to her brother just how little they had, and how there wasn't anything more to sell to put a single meal on the table each day.

"He was bound to provide better, by your father's will," Mrs. Erics muttered, repeating the words she had each time Jerry's name came up. "Your father worked hard to provide for the two of you. Isn't right he's taken most of it. Even worse that he sold the house, no thought to what would happen to you."

"No, it's not right, but what can I do?" Sage asked. "Nothing. I suppose Jerry did give us warning a few months ago that the house was to be sold, so that's something."

She sighed softly, then opened the letter reluctantly. "Might as well get this over with."

Sage didn't want to verbalize that she felt the shame of not being able to have found a way out of their situation. The housekeeper would have scolded her, and though Sage knew the woman would have been right, that it wasn't her fault, there was no one else to shoulder the responsibility.

Mrs. Erics busied herself dishing out the soup and setting it on the table. The painful ache in Sage's stomach—part apprehension over the letter and a good deal more of a ceaseless hunger—nearly burned. Sage unfolded the letter and then squeezed her eyes shut to block sight of the short missive. As always, Jerry was to the point. Sage was surprised he'd even bothered to write her, and to pay for the postage to send it.

"That didn't take long. What's your brother's excuse this time?" the housekeeper asked.

There was no sorrow in Sage. No hurt. No surprise. For there to have been any of those things, there had to have been hope, and that was something she'd not had for a very long time.

She shook her head, and indicated the letter. "He didn't have one. Just said he couldn't help."

The older woman sniffed. "He's likely used them all up and can't think of any more." Then her eyes softened. "I'm sorry, my dear. What will you do now?"

"Give you another chance to leave," Sage said quietly. "To seek employment with another family, where you will have a roof over your head and three meals a day."

"I have already told you, that isn't going to happen," Mrs. Erics said, her voice firm. "Perhaps you'll get another letter soon, one from that mail-order agency you applied to."

"Yes, that might happen," Sage said, trying to sound hopeful, though she felt anything but. Truthfully, she'd forgotten all about her letter to the Garden Belles. Sent one day in pure desperation, she'd not heard anything back and assumed either it was lost in the mailing or that they didn't have anyone for her.

"Has Jerry at least offered to let you live there with him and his wife?" Mrs. Erics asked.

"Of course not. That would cost Lorelei money," Sage said with a bitter laugh.

She tried not to let anger bubble up, but all she could think about was how her brother had married a gold digger who was determined to squeeze every ounce from him.

I wonder if she realizes he's worth far less than she first thought? Why, he might be surviving off of promises to others and hopes himself.

"No matter. We will figure it out. Did I tell you little Wendy Baker's cat has just had a litter of kittens?"

Mrs. Erics changed the subject and began to chatter, but Sage wasn't paying attention, even though the idea of baby kittens would have usually enthralled her. She couldn't think about anything but their dire situation. Though her beloved friend, who had been by her side since the day she was born, put on an air of confidence that all was well, Sage knew it wasn't. And, she was feeling just as responsible for their situation as Mrs. Erics seemed to feel.

Sage's eyes wandered over the house, the place that had sheltered her for her entire life. The place she knew, had offered protection, and was nearly empty, with most everything having been sold off to provide for them since her father passed away and her brother left home.

Where there had once been rows of books, and lovely paintings and even a good number of household goods like linens and dishes, all but the bare necessities were long gone.

Mrs. Erics's words spun around and around in her head as her eyes fell on Jerry's letter again. What would she do now? That indeed was the question. What could she do? She had nothing at all she could do anything *with*.

Chapter 3

"Micah, I warned you that if you didn't take this seriously, I'd handle matters myself." His mother looked at him cooly over her teacup. "The young woman sounds perfectly suitable."

"Suitable," Micah repeated dryly. "That's just what I'm looking for in a wife. Never mind the other features I'd like. Or, heaven forbid, affection or love."

"Nothing was or is stopping you from such a thing," his mother answered sternly. "Nothing except for yourself, that is. You've known for the last four years that the day would come and you'd need to marry. You are now twenty-five, Micah. Time is almost up for you to marry before your birthday."

When he started to protest, she continued, "You've had ample opportunities to find a young woman you like. But, you have not, and I will not see the business your father built up for you in the hands of a relative who might drive it into the ground, someone who has not put an ounce of sweat or effort into the company, all because you don't marry and complete the terms in his will!"

The will. It seemed to Micah that since his father had passed away nearly eight years ago, he'd lived in fear of the will. It had dictated each move he had made in running the railway company. Dictated that he must marry. And though he'd tried his best to push that out of the way, it had crept up on him, and the time was nearly here.

Though he'd never admit it, there was no one who had caught his attention, and this decision by his mother, as terrible as it sounded, was a practical one. Even if he hated it.

Micah turned from the window to face his mother, who was staring at him, her brows arched.

"Yes, but a stranger, Mother? We know nothing about her! Aren't you concerned she might be only after my money? A woman with a past? Or even some sort of criminal?" Micah rubbed his jaw in frustration. Perhaps a little concern as well. He didn't want to invite something like that into his home and put his mother in danger.

"Yes, I was," his mother answered, calmly taking a sip of her tea. "But not only is this agency pristine in reputation, I also hired a detective to learn a little more about her. She is as the letter states. A sweet, hardworking young woman who has fallen on difficult times. She has, however, also never asked for anything from anyone. I have no reason to believe she will present as anything more. Nor do you."

"And this is supposed to make me feel better?" Micah asked. "Now I'm supposed to feel sorry for her because she's fallen on hard times, and only I can help her? What if I don't like her?"

"Really, Micah," his mother chided him. "I've never known you to be so excitable. It's simple, really. Don't make things so complicated sounding." She set her tea down and gestured to the letter.

"When she arrives in two weeks, we will put her up at the hotel for a time. That gives you a chance to get to know her. If you really loathe her, then we will apologize and I will pay for her to travel elsewhere while requesting another bride from the Garden Belles. I'm sure I could even find someone for the girl to marry. However, should you like each other, then that's wonderful. I didn't mention we have money, other than that you'd be able to provide for her. So, that's one less worry. I kept the details about you to a bare minimum."

Micah sat down heavily. "You make this sound so transactional," he said. "As though we are picking her out from the store, looking her over carefully first to see if she's suitable, like you might a dress or a horse or a pie."

"It didn't have to be that way," his mother answered him softly, "however, you made it so by delaying."

"And this is to be my punishment?" Some of the anger had left Micah, but not all of it. He knew he'd had the chance to choose. He still had time! This wasn't fair. Why, he could march into town this very moment and—

No, no he couldn't. There wasn't anyone he'd even consider there. And his mother knew it. She also knew that by sending away for someone, she'd be coming because she wanted Micah, not a man who owned a railway company. That's why she was so confident the woman wouldn't take advantage of them.

"It's not a punishment," his mother said, a hard edge coming into her voice. Her eyes fixed on him, steel in her gaze. "Your father—"

Micah stood and held out a hand to stop her. He knew the conversation was over. There was nothing more he could do. "Fine. I will do this your way. However, you must promise if, by some chance, I find another woman, one I do like, you'll respect that."

"Why, of course I will," his mother sniffed. "You act like I'm not giving you any say. I always have."

That was only half true. Yes, she'd always given him say...but she often made the choices, and so even when he picked between them, it wasn't a decision he might have made himself. That, to Micah, was practically the same as not getting to choose at all.

"So I've your word?" Micah asked.

"Yes." His mother stood and embraced him. "I'm sorry, my darling, that this has upset you. I'm sure, however, this Miss Robinson will be well suited to be your wife. And—" she added, seeing Micah was about to protest, "you have my word if you find someone else, you've my blessing there as well. Truthfully, my dear, I'd rather see you happily wed than not, but with so little time..." She shook her head, and closed her eyes for a moment. When she opened them, she added, "But I know you'll do the right thing. And no matter your choice, we will both do the right thing by Miss Robinson, and see her looked after while she finds a new husband."

The right thing. How those words galled him. Hadn't he always done that? As long as Micah could remember, he'd always thought of others, done what they needed, be it his parents or the railway's shareholders, even if he hadn't wanted to, like all of the events he'd hosted. Why would this be any different? Even if he was protesting, Micah knew in the end what would happen. He'd be married.

Micah knew there was nothing he could say to counter that argument. His mother was completely correct. As she usually was. If he wasn't married, he'd lose the business his father had built from the ground up. He couldn't do that. His family had sacrificed. Wealth was slowly built, they were from humble origins and now quite comfortable, and Micah wouldn't let their sacrifices be for nothing.

She left the room then, leaving the letter she'd pointed to on the small table next to her empty teacup. Micah picked it up and scanned the letter. Miss Robinson. He wished he knew more. What was her first name? Would he like it? Would he like her? What did she look like? What of the things she enjoyed? Was there even such a thing as a successful love match with a stranger?

Micah didn't know, but with his last question he was sure it wasn't possible. When you didn't choose for yourself, and a spouse was thrust upon you, how could that ever happen? He dropped his head into his hands, feeling sorry for himself, and the young woman who was likely on her way, excited for her future.

Chapter 4

Sage pushed back the strand of blonde hair that had escaped her braid, and adjusted the brim of her worn hat to block the sun just a little better.

It was just midmorning, but she'd visited every place in town that might be hiring. None were. By the sixth place, it was all she could do not to show her distress. She'd smiled, kept her chin up, but the weight on her shoulders felt so heavy, Sage wasn't sure how much longer she could do that.

It didn't matter, though. There was no other choice. She had to do something. Even finding a job right now wouldn't fix their situation, not if it didn't provide enough for them to have a roof over their heads. She revisited the idea of living in the woods, making some sort of a tent perhaps, and then saving up until they could find a room to rent. Would that be possible? Sage shook her head. No. She couldn't ask Mrs. Erics to do such a thing.

"Miss Robinson?"

Sage turned, glancing around for who had called her name, and saw the postmaster waving from the small post office. She walked closer.

"Hello, Mr. Martin," she said. "Were you calling me?"

"Yes, you got a letter," he told her. "One moment."

Sage furrowed her brow. A letter? Who would have written? It wasn't likely it would have been her brother. One had just arrived from him, and that would be most unlike Jerry. She watched as the man rifled through a mail slot, then pulled free an envelope.

As he slid it toward her and her gaze fell on the sender, something Sage hadn't felt for so long she was surprised she even recognized it sparked within her.

Hope.

With trembling fingers, she reached for the envelope and whispered, "Thank you, Mr. Martin."

His farewell was lost as she walked away, almost as though in a trance. There was a letter from the Garden Belles. More than that...the letter was thick. Could that mean...Dare she even hope?

Sage thought of tearing it open right then, but if this was to be her salvation, she didn't want to risk something happening to the letter. It would be better to open it at home. And, if it were not to be, she'd have Mrs. Erics to console her because Sage was at the absolute end of what she could bear without a good cry.

Hurriedly, she turned on the path that led the about ten minutes of a brisk walk to her home. The whole way, Sage held the letter tightly, scared it might blow away, or else worse—that she was imagining it.

As the house appeared, she broke into a run. "Mrs. Erics!" she called, bursting in through the front door. "Mrs. Erics!"

The housekeeper came rushing into the front foyer. "What's wrong?" she gasped. "What's happened?"

"A letter," Sage said, holding it out. "It's from the mail-order marriage agency." Then she realized the woman had likely thought the worst. "I'm sorry. I didn't mean to frighten you. I'm just...I don't know what to think. I'm scared to open it, truthfully." She began to tremble.

"Don't be," Mrs. Erics said. "This could be something wonderful."

"I know you are right," Sage said, trying to loosen her grip on the envelope, "but what if it isn't? I don't think I can handle any more bad news."

"Do you want to wait to open it?" Mrs. Erics asked.

Sage drew in a deep breath, released it, and shook her head. "No." She slid her finger along the back of the envelope, and pulled out the thick bundle. "What is all of this?" she asked.

"What looks to be a small fortune," Mrs. Erics gasped, as money slid from Sage's grasp and fluttered to the hardwood beneath their feet. She stooped to pick it up, her expression one of shock.

"And train tickets!" Sage said. "One for each of us!"

"Read the letter," Mrs. Erics ordered. "So we have an explanation of what this all is!"

Sage nodded and unfolded the letter. She read,

Dear Miss Robinson,

We are delighted to tell you that we have found a potential husband for you. His name is Mr. Walker. He has enclosed these train tickets and money for you and your companion's travel expenses as you travel to Kansas.

Sage stopped reading and looked up at Mrs. Erics. "I can hardly believe it."

"Does it say anything more about the man?" the housekeeper asked, looking at the letter.

"No. This letter is short and to the point." Sage worried at a fingernail. "Does that mean he's an awful person, do you think?"

"I don't," the housekeeper said. "It could be he didn't tell them much about himself. But, just to be on the safe side, we will plan to find a place to stay for a few days while you make his acquaintance. If you dislike him, then we will simply figure out something else to do. Perhaps seek employment in that new town, or write to them and ask for a new husband."

"You are right," Sage said firmly. "That's just what we will do. If nothing else, it gets us to a different town, and one where there might be a future for us." She glanced at the train tickets. "How fortunate we are. The timing couldn't be better. But what if he doesn't let us stay together?"

Mrs. Erics pulled Sage into a tight embrace. "Then, my dear, I will be quite fine on my own. You are grown; you don't still need me."

"Yes, I do," Sage whispered. "I will always need you. I love you."

She could feel the shudder as Mrs. Erics suppressed a sob. "And I will always love you," the other woman told her. "But let us try not to worry about the future further than we must," she said. "I have the feeling," she added, pulling back to smile broadly at Sage, "things are going to work out splendidly. However, we need to pack."

"You are right," Sage said, and glanced around. "We've so little time."

"Then we had best get started," Mrs. Erics said. "Luckily, we've little to bring. That will be a blessing. Less to carry! I wonder what Kansas will be like. I've never been there myself."

"I wonder too," Sage said. "It is bound to be different. Perhaps that's just what we need." She tried to smile bravely; Mrs. Erics was being so confident and she wished she could be the same, but Sage was sure her lips wobbled.

Mrs. Erics hadn't seemed to notice, though, as she glanced around the kitchen. "I wonder what I should bring. I will admit, the things I'll miss aren't those I can take. Like the tree outside."

"I will miss that too," Sage said. "It was lovely to sit under and read. Or climb, when I—and it—was much smaller."

The housekeeper laughed. "How could I forget? All those torn dresses." She shook her head. "No matter. All right. Time is wasting. I'm going to get started."

"Wait," Sage told her. She took one of the train tickets and handed it to her, along with half of the money.

"My dear, this is for you," Mrs. Erics said, trying to hand back the money.

"It is for our travel expenses," Sage corrected her. "And while I am sure neither of us will use more than necessary, I think it best if one of us doesn't carry the whole of it. In case it is lost or stolen."

"You are right on that," Mrs. Erics said. She grew a thoughtful look. "Will you wear your spring green travel dress?"

"I suppose so," Sage said, a little in surprise. "It's older to be sure, but quite serviceable. But why?"

"I will cut into the lining," Mrs. Erics said. "There, I will hide part of the money. I will do the same with my travel dress. Then, if our handbags are lost or stolen, we are not completely at the mercy of strangers."

"What a wonderful idea," Sage said. "I'll fetch my dress. Tomorrow, I will walk to town, and use a small portion for some supplies so that we can make bread for our journey."

She hurried up the stairs to her room and went to the wardrobe. It was nearly bare. She hadn't had a new dress since her father had passed away, and some of them were getting quite thin and ratty. It would be hard to choose her best dress to wear for her future husband, but hopefully he would understand.

It was then Sage realized she didn't know what the man did for a living. Was he a farmer? If so, her dresses would be quite fine, and perhaps he'd consent to giving her money for fabric for a Sunday best dress. Then, she looked down at the money still tight in her grasp. Surely no farmer would have that much. This was quite ample. In fact, more than.

A thought flitted through her mind, wondering if she had time to be so frivolous as to get fabric for a new dress, taking part of these funds her future husband had sent. But what if they didn't get along? No, she couldn't spend a penny more than was necessary, as she'd be bound to return what wasn't used, and as they were not married, didn't dare to use anything beyond travel expenses. Surely, though, he wouldn't object to her spending a little for food.

Sage nodded briskly. She'd simply buy the flour, and perhaps a few apples. Maybe a small wedge of cheese. It had been so long since she'd had any, and that was a good thing to travel with.

Hurriedly, Sage gathered her travel dress and the money and returned downstairs, heading to the kitchen where Mrs. Erics had laid out her sewing supplies.

"Split the money however you think best," Sage told the housekeeper, "with some sewn in, the rest for our handbags."

The housekeeper nodded. "I will. Now, you go pack. After dinner, I will do the same."

Sage nodded, and then stopped and whispered, "It seems to all be happening so quickly, doesn't it? It felt like I'd been waiting forever for a reply, and now..." She drew in a deep breath. "I always thought I'd have time to get to know the one I was to marry. That he'd be someone I liked. Loved. Had time to know."

"It's funny how things work out," Mrs. Erics agreed. "However, just because you may not have those things this time doesn't mean that you won't grow to like or love your husband. Remember, we will not stay and you will not marry if he's not someone you could see yourself with."

Sage nodded, and left the kitchen, returning to her room. She moved hastily, not to pack, but to hide the tears slipping down her cheeks. Mrs. Erics had tried to reassure her, but Sage knew she'd never be able to turn down the offer of marriage, especially if the man would let Mrs. Erics stay with her. She felt such a responsibility toward the woman.

Beyond that, they were desperate. They had nothing. There were no other options, and unless it was obvious that the man would beat her or use her as a slave, Sage knew she'd have to say yes.

Indeed, it was funny how things worked out sometimes, but the idea of an arranged marriage…it wasn't the least bit funny to her at all. It was frightening.

Chapter 5

How was it that soon he could be a married man, and without any of the usual ways of going about it? The catching of someone's eye, the shy smiles, the stomach spinning wildly as he asked if he could call on her. At least, Micah thought that was how it was supposed to go.

Micah studied himself in the hotel room mirror, wondering how his future had come to this. It was his own fault; he knew that it was. He hadn't really made much of an effort, but...a stranger? Had he realized that he'd have to marry a stranger in order to be sure he met the will's deadline, he'd have likely put forth more of an effort to meet someone he could settle for.

With a heavy sigh, he picked up his travel bag, and then the second one with the contract and other business papers he'd been sent this way to sign, and left the room, closing the door gently behind him.

"Good morning, Mr. Walker!" the hotel manager said. "See you next time."

"See you then," Micah said with a sort of wave, as he juggled the bags in his hand. He'd stayed at this hotel at least twice a year since he took over the railway business. It was clean, comfortable, and only a short distance from the station. He had quickly learned his favorite places to stay at, and this was one of them.

As he stepped out onto the sidewalk, Micah couldn't help but admire the sky. The blue was incredible, the sun was shining brightly, and all the world seemed happy and content. A strange contrast to the worry and discomfort inside him as he wondered just what the woman he was going to marry would be like.

Would they get along? Would he like her? Would he be able to love her? She was coming with a companion, the letter had said. A chaperone, he assumed. What would that person be like? Younger? Older? Fussy? Demanding? Would his potential bride be that way herself?

Oh, Micah knew he shouldn't think such things. He ought not to make up his mind about the young woman—at least he hoped she was around his age—before he met her, but it was rather hard, when the letter from the mail-order bride agency had been so scant on details.

"Welcome aboard, sir," the conductor said, and Micah nodded.

"Thank you. And, remember, please. While I'm on the train, it's just Micah."

"Of course, sir," the conductor said. "You know your way to the car."

He did. Though Micah could have traveled in a private compartment, he liked to sit in the main part of the carriage, so that he could hear any concerns or compliments about the train and the service the passengers had. If there was a reasonable way to improve their experiences, he wanted to do so. It was also a good way to make sure the conductors who didn't know who he was treated the passengers politely and professionally, and that the railcars were kept as clean as reasonably possible.

Micah settled into his seat and opened the newspaper he'd bought on the way. As the train rolled away from the station, he got himself caught up on the news. Time passed quickly, and about an hour later, the train paused at the next station. Micah glanced through the window to see how many passengers were to get on the train, when two in particular caught his eye.

Almost timidly, a young woman around his age and another woman, who appeared to perhaps be her mother, hesitantly approached a conductor. The conductor nodded, and gestured to the railcar. Micah watched as he offered to take the rather shabby bags the women held, but both shook their heads and clutched them tightly.

The women climbed the small steps and into the nearly empty railcar. Micah started to resume his newspaper when the younger of the two's voices caught his attention.

"What do we do now, do you think?" she asked her companion.

"I'm not sure," the other woman answered. "I don't think we have assigned seats?"

Micah quickly stood. "Hello," he offered in a friendly tone. "I couldn't help but overhear. No, there are no assigned seats in this car. You may sit wherever you like."

"Oh! That's a relief," the younger woman said. "We've never been on a train before, and don't quite know how it all works."

"Would you like to sit here?" Micah asked, indicating the bench opposite of his. "I'd be happy to answer any questions you might have. I travel a good deal."

"That would be lovely," the older woman said. She settled herself onto the bench, sliding closest to the window. "I'm Mrs. Erics."

"I'm Sage," the younger woman said.

"And I'm Micah," he told them, taking his own seat.

Sage shyly asked, "You are sure it's not a bother to answer a few questions?"

"Not a bit of it," he assured her. "It would be my honor."

Just then, the train's whistle, loud and long, sounded. Sage and Mrs. Erics both gasped and startled.

"My word," the older woman said, a hand at her throat. "How often will it make that noise?"

It was all Micah could do not to laugh. "Not too often," he reassured her. "It will make the sound as we approach each station, and before we leave to warn the passengers, then once more as we leave."

Sage reached into her handbag, and pulled out her tickets. "Do you know how many stations we will pass through? I want to keep count so we don't miss ours."

"May I see?" Micah asked. When she nodded and offered him the tickets, he looked at her in surprise. "That's my destination as well. Let's see, it will take about two days to get there. I couldn't tell you exactly how many stations. Sometimes I sleep through a few of them, but you've no fear of missing your stop. The conductor will warn you, and I will as well."

"Now that is providence," Mrs. Erics proclaimed. "How fortunate we are!"

"Indeed," Sage said, relief on her face.

Micah tried not to study her, but he was curious. Now that they were so near to him, he saw it wasn't just their bags, now tucked under their seats, that looked worn, but also their clothing. Both were clean and neat, but it was clear that their dresses were older. It was obvious, too, that they were not related. Sage had blonde hair, Mrs. Erics, though it was graying, had dark hair.

The train sounded the whistle once more, and started to pull away from the station. Sage and Mrs. Erics grabbed on to each other as the train jolted forward.

When she caught him looking at her, Sage turned a bright red. "Forgive us," she said. "We are rather inexperienced with trains."

"You'll be an expert soon," Micah assured her. "In fact, it won't be much longer before the whistle no longer startles you, and you simply enjoy the tone."

"I think I already do," Sage said, leaning eagerly toward the window. Then, her face clouded, and she said to her companion, so softly he could hardly hear it, "How quickly it is all moving away. Mrs. Erics, do you think I will ever get to return home?"

He couldn't hear the reply, but the sorrow on the faces of the two women filled Micah with a pain he hadn't expected to feel.

Micah tried to turn back to his newspaper, give them a sense of privacy for their conversation, but his mind kept wandering to the young woman across from him and the tear he saw rolling down her cheek unnoticed, as her eyes were fixed on the swiftly moving scenery.

For some reason Micah couldn't explain, he longed to comfort her. But that wouldn't have been appropriate. Neither would the strange desire he had to get to know her better. Soon, he'd be a married man, and it would be best if he didn't think about the lovely blonde woman across from him, the one with the sweet voice, the beautiful eyes, and the sadness she couldn't hide.

Chapter 6

The first few hours on the train passed easily enough. Sage found that it was as Micah said, and she did get used to the abrupt whistle of the train, and the way it shuddered coming to a stop or jolting to a start. She was grateful that he sat across from them, ready to answer any questions they had and set their minds at ease.

Sage was a little nervous, and hoped she was hiding it well. Though she'd relaxed slightly since she'd gotten on the train, there was a good deal to be worried about that kept her from fully relaxing, like she noticed so many others doing.

Things like train accidents and robbers.

"Micah?" Sage ventured quietly.

He looked over at once, his warm eyes finding hers immediately. "How can I help you?"

She flushed slightly, but asked, "How often do train accidents happen? Or robberies?"

Understanding washed over his face. She felt relieved he wasn't looking judgmental. Earnestly, he said, "I can promise you that in my years of riding the train, I have never experienced a robbery nor an accident. The railway actually has a detective ride the train to help keep it safe."

"Do they? That makes me feel a little better," Sage said. "I appreciate you not making me feel silly for asking."

"You can ask anything you'd like," Micah told her. "I won't think you are silly at all."

The train slowed, coming to its screeching stop before a station. Sage watched as a woman a few rows in front of them jumped up and dashed off the train. "Oh no! She's left her bag," Sage said, starting to rise to chase after the woman and call her back. With some luck, she could toss it to her before the train left.

"It's okay, she hasn't," Micah said, stopping her, and pointed through the window. "She's just buying something and then she'll return until her destination."

"Buying something?" Sage frowned.

"Here, if you don't mind sharing my row for a moment," Micah said, moving as far to the train's side as he could against the window, "you'll see better."

Hesitating, and glancing quickly at Mrs. Erics, who was somehow able to doze, she nodded, and slid on the bench next to him. Through his side of the window,

Sage witnessed a flurry of activity. And it was just as he'd said. The woman who'd left the train was returning, with something wrapped in brown paper. As Sage studied the scene before her, she saw a young boy holding a bundle of newspapers, and several men and women with baskets of fruit, small loaves of bread, and wrapped bundles she assumed were also food items of sorts.

The woman in their train car hadn't been the only one to get something and then rush back to the train. Just the sight made Sage's stomach ache with hunger. She ignored it, though, something she was good at.

"You see, when the train stops, the passengers are allowed to leave if they want to get a newspaper or something to eat. Do you see all of those people?" he asked, gesturing to a number of people walking around with baskets. "They sell goods. Some stops are longer than others, but as long as they climb back on before the train leaves, it's quite normal for passengers to step onto the platform."

"Oh! I see!" Sage said. She bit her lip and ventured, "So at the next stop, I would have time to fetch something for Mrs. Erics and myself?"

Micah nodded. "The next stop would be ideal. You'd have almost ten minutes."

"Then that's just what I'll do," Sage said. "Thank you."

The train started to move, and Sage wondered if she should return to her seat. Micah hadn't said anything, and she enjoyed sitting near him, but what was the right thing to do?

Luckily, Micah started talking, and she let herself be distracted from her worries.

"Are you enjoying yourself so far?" he asked.

Sage nodded. "I am. Now that I am used to the movement and the noise, it's much less worrying. We go so quickly, it's an absolute marvel."

"It really is," Micah said. "Why, travel by rail has really revolutionized the country. It's incredible how much we can see, and how fast we can get there. It's my preferred method of travel, and much nicer than going by stagecoach."

"That's something else I've never done," Sage said. "Honestly, I've never been much of anywhere. I don't know if I'll ever have the chance to do so again, so I'm trying to enjoy each moment. That's been easy to do, really."

"Might I ask what brings you to travel to Kansas?" Micah asked.

Sage hesitated, then nodded. "I'm...I'm to be married. I think."

Was it her imagination, or had the smile he wore faltered slightly?

"Is that so? Congratulations," Micah said. Then he frowned and scratched his head. "Wait, what do you mean, you think? If that's not being impolite to ask," he hastily added.

Sage twisted her hands in her lap. "Well, I'm not quite sure, as I'm a mail-order bride," Sage said, the words absolutely mortifying, though they released anyway. "I have no other option, I'm afraid." She tried to smile, as though her fears didn't exist, but her lips just wouldn't curve.

"Is that so?" Micah said softly. "I'm sorry."

They sat quietly. Sage wondered if she should explain more, but she really didn't want to. Selfishly, she wanted to pretend that she was something she was not. An ordinary traveler, meeting and enjoying the company of a gentleman, and not a woman who had left everything she had behind in order to survive.

How difficult life could be without bread for your belly or clothing on your back, and a bit of shelter to call one's own. Sage hadn't realized it at first. While her father was alive, she'd wanted for nothing. But as soon as he'd passed away, and her brother both wed and assumed control over the family finances, things had grown very difficult.

Never had Sage imagined she would be forced to take such drastic steps to ensure her future. But with no means to provide for herself and Mrs. Erics—and not for lack of trying—there was nothing more to do. She supposed she ought to feel grateful that she could have such a thing as a man willing to accept her into his life without knowing anything about her.

But the truth remained, she was very frightened. She was also very concerned. Sage had never had the opportunity to pass the time with someone who was as interesting or as pleasing to her as Micah was. It had awakened within her not only the desire to spend more time with him but also a fear.

Here she was, on her way to become a married woman. Was she making a mistake? Had she really exhausted all options to her before choosing a mail-order marriage?

"I'm very glad that we've met," Micah's warm voice said, breaking into her thoughts. "You've made my trip much more enjoyable."

Her face broke into a smile. She couldn't help it. "You've done the same for me," she said.

And as the train slowed, and Sage and Mrs. Erics hurried off to buy some sustenance as cheaply as possible, with Micah's promise to stand guard over their bags and keep the train from departing, Sage couldn't stop thinking about how much she liked him, and how she trusted him.

Dare she hope to feel that sort of connection with her future husband? It was luck indeed that they were traveling to the same place. Maybe if her promised match was dreadful she could spend a little more time with Micah.

But just as soon as she thought that, Sage knew such a thing could never be. No matter how horrible the man was that she was to marry, she simply must. There were no other options, and she needed to do all she could to care for Mrs. Erics, who had selflessly taken care of Sage, even though she didn't have to.

The train whistle sounded a warning, and Sage and Mrs. Erics hurried over to the step. Micah was waiting there, and offered his hand to her. As she took it, feeling the warmth of his touch and a sense of comfort and rightness, Sage suddenly found herself blinking back tears.

Why, oh why, had she had to meet Micah? It would make marrying whoever she was to wed all the more difficult.

Chapter 7

The scenery sped by. There were fields and forests, small buildings that dotted the landscape. At a distance, cattle roamed and a cowboy rode on a horse with his dog, herding them into another pasture. If Micah were to look upward, he'd see the bright blue sky, with no clouds to keep the sun from shining brightly. All of it was beautiful, but none compared to Sage.

Why was it only now, Micah thought, that he'd found someone he was interested in? And, there wasn't just the complication of him about to be married, with his own mail-order spouse on the way, but she was to be one as well! Life sure had a way of playing tricks on people.

Micah wished—more than wished—that it was Sage on her way to be with him. It would ease some of the ache he was feeling, that stabbing of his heart about to crack, when he realized that neither were in a position to do more than be friends, and he hated it.

It was a silly thought, however. Micah knew he wouldn't be so fortunate to get anyone half as wonderful as Sage was. He just hoped, for her sake, the man she was to marry would cherish her in the way she deserved.

It was obvious that Sage was holding back something, the thing that was forcing her to become a mail-order bride. He was a stranger, almost, so he didn't blame her for not telling him. However, he couldn't help but feel concern. Was she in danger? Or dire straits? It was obvious there was some sort of a situation that was making her desperate to marry, and a stranger no less. Was there anything he could do to help them?

He studied her as she and Mrs. Erics talked quietly from their seats across from him. Each had been nibbling at a single roll most of the day, having only left the train to buy water. He couldn't imagine that they weren't hungry. Famished, even. Was that why the marriage?

Could it be her finances? Why else would a woman as lovely as she was have to consider such a thing as a marriage by mail? Had no one in her town showered her with attention and offers of protection or help? He would have.

Oh, yes, Micah knew there was far more to choosing the person you wanted to spend your life with than simply looks, but Sage also had a lovely disposition, seemed clever, and her laugh...her smile... Micah was sure there had never been anything so wonderful to hear or see.

What would it be like to hear that every day for the rest of his life? Heaven, that's what.

But he needed to stop thinking such things. It wasn't the least bit fair to himself or to the woman who was traveling to wed him.

Across the aisle, Sage glanced over, and her beautiful smile landed on him. Mrs. Erics said something, pointing through the window, and her attention returned to the older woman.

Micah wondered about her as well. Were they friends? Had they known each other long? It seemed it, by the way they were so comfortable together and how Mrs. Erics seemed so protective of her.

He let his eyes roam around the carriage. The passengers were doing the usual things. Dozing, reading. A woman near the front was sewing, and a man across from her was writing something. Everyone seemed occupied.

Micah wished he could find a way to keep his own restless thoughts from tormenting him. He couldn't keep staring at Sage. It wouldn't be proper. And it might upset her. Yet, it was hard not to think about her. When he tried to read, he couldn't concentrate.

With a sigh, he turned to the window again. Trees, patchy in spots, grew denser. He knew this area. There would be a few miles of trees and then a small town.

He had stayed there a few times. The hotel was a good one, larger than some he'd been to, and with a restaurant attached.

From the corner of his eye, Micah caught a flicker of movement and squinted, turning his head. There was a man on a horse riding along the train. No, there were two. Three. More than that! Each was waving a cloth, as though trying to warn the train to stop. There must be danger ahead!

Rising from his seat, Micah had one thought. To seek out the detective on board. The man would be in the car in front of them. Hopefully, he'd noticed the riders. Micah couldn't take the chance, though. This was his railway, his railcar. He needed to do what he could.

If he couldn't find the detective, he'd make his way to the engineer, to warn the man something might be amiss. Hopefully, he'd make it in time. He could see the riders urging their horses faster, but they were no match for the train's speed.

Micah had nearly reached the door that connected this car to the one before him. A curve in the track was ahead, and the train would slow. Perhaps the conductor or the engineer would catch sight of the warning. He hoped so. There was no way he'd be able to reach them quickly. All he could do was try.

Sage caught sight of him, and their eyes locked. She opened her mouth as though to ask him what he was doing, when the train suddenly gave a horrible jolt as it slowed at an alarming rate. The train's brakes shrieked in an alarming way. There were screams from the car, and objects flew through the air. Someone's bag slid into the narrow pathway and opened, spilling the contents on the ground.

The train jolted once more, much harder this time, and swayed dangerously. Micah found himself flying through the air.

Chapter 8

Sage's brows furrowed. She'd only glanced over, but there was a look on Micah's face that concerned her, and she watched as he swiftly rose from his seat. She wanted to ask if he was unwell or if something was wrong, but then everything happened at once.

The train slowed rapidly, gave a horrible shudder unlike what she'd experienced thus far, and then it swayed and jerked to a sudden halt. A scream tore from her lips as she lurched forward, striking the bench before her. As she tried to catch herself, her eyes landed on Micah as he flew into the air, and then landed on the train's floor in a heap.

What had happened? Had the train wrecked? Sage glanced around in a panic. She could see a man approaching from outside, trying to force the door open. He must have come to assist the train.

"Thank goodness," Mrs. Erics said shakily. "Help already. Are you hurt?"

"No," Sage said, surprised it was so. "But Micah might be." She started toward him, when he managed to pull himself to standing and then held his hands up in front of him.

Sage felt confused at the gesture, until she saw why he'd done that. The man whom she thought had been rushing to help them had a far different plan. She could see him better now; the hat pulled low, a bandana over the lower part of his face, and only his eyes peeking through the narrow slit.

One hand held a sack, the other a gun. Sage sucked in her breath. Micah's eyes darted to hers, and he took a half step toward her before the man snarled.

"Don't move, or I'll kill someone. Nice and slow, just drop your money, jewelry, watches, and other valuables in the sack," the man said, his voice rough and raspy. He fixed his gaze on Micah. "Don't go being a hero, boy. I'll kill everyone but you, just so you suffer. Mark my words."

Sage believed him. It appeared Micah did too. She wondered if the other train cars were being robbed at the same time. Swallowing hard, she watched as Micah reached into his pocket and dropped his money into the sack. Satisfied, the man continued on his way.

Row by row, he made his way closer to her and Mrs. Erics. Sage watched as watches and rings, necklaces and money were dropped into the sack. It was all that she could do not to touch her secret pocket. How grateful she was that Mrs. Erics had sewed them in to protect the majority of their money! In fact, still anxious to carry much, Sage had put even more in the bottom of her bag, leaving only a handful of dollars that she could easily reach.

The robber stopped, his eyes looking at her expectantly. Sage reached into her handbag, letting her elbow deliberately strike Mrs. Erics in warning. She pulled out the few dollars and some coins. Sage's trembling voice said, "This is all we have, sir. All of it."

He studied her, as though she might be lying, and Sage allowed her shame to bubble to the surface, to hopefully convince him to look no further. Her cheeks blazed, and Sage hoped that it added to her convincingness. She held out the money and whispered, "The man I am to marry from the mail-order marriage agency sent it for our travel expenses. We've no jewelry. Everything was sold long ago when my father died."

The robber's eyes flicked from the paltry amount to her and Mrs. Erics. His eyes were cold, uncaring. But he seemed to believe her and gave a short nod. "Drop it in," he said, and when Sage had, continued to the next person.

As Micah stepped toward her, the robber let off a warning shot. It echoed through the carriage, and most everyone screamed or ducked. Sage found herself tightly in Mrs. Erics's arms.

"I told you," the robber said calmly, looking at Micah, "No heroes. She'll be the first to get it if anyone moves." He pointed his gun toward her.

Sage met Micah's eyes. She could tell how upset he was. How much he wanted to move, but didn't want to risk her getting hurt. Even though they were in a terrible situation, the fact that he wanted to protect her warmed her slightly. Her heart was pounding, and while it was difficult to say if it was from fear or Micah, it didn't really matter. She didn't want him to get hurt, but welcomed the thought behind his action.

The robber spoke, and all eyes turned to his. "Thank you, folks. Once the tracks are repaired, I'm sure you'll continue along." He pushed his way back to the door and jumped out. A moment later, he and several other men thundered away on horses.

The tracks. So they had done something to them. Sage was scared, but she supposed she was also grateful. A good number of lives could have been lost had the train not stopped how it had. What if they'd been going over a ravine, with no bridge?

The second the robber was out the door and mounting his horse, Micah had rushed to Sage. Before she quite realized what was happening, he had put his hands on her elbows.

"Are you hurt?" he asked, his eyes frantically moving over her.

"No, I'm not," Sage assured him. "But you, you've a terrible bruise forming." She lifted her hand gently to his forehead. "It looks worrying."

"It doesn't matter. As long as you aren't hurt," Micah said. He glanced around. "I must speak with the rail detective."

He released her, much to her disappointment, and called out, "Everyone, please remain here. I'm going to get the railway detective and check on the conductor and engineer."

Sage watched anxiously as he stepped through the connecting train car doors. Mrs. Erics had pulled their bags from under the seat and set them on the bench. A woman stepped forward, collecting her belongings that had spilled out, and Sage stooped to help her.

"What will we do now?" Sage asked once she'd returned to her seat. "How will we get where we need to go?"

"I don't know," Mrs. Erics said, her face grim. "But we are fortunate that Micah has been able to answer each question so far. We will simply have to beg his assistance in this as well."

"No begging is required," Micah said, his voice warm and reassuring as he suddenly appeared at her elbow. "Don't worry."

He spoke louder then, getting everyone in the railcar's attention. "There is a town about three miles away. We will need to walk there. If you've a medical need, you'll stay here with some of the rail staff. We can send for a wagon to retrieve you once we are there. The railway company will pay for your lodgings and meals, and arrange for your travel to your final destination by stage or train, from the next town."

"Are you sure?" Sage asked, concern filling her. "Is the town large enough? Aren't there too many passengers? And the cost!"

"That's the rail's responsibility," Micah said.

"I've never heard such a thing," Mrs. Erics protested. "It was a robber, not an accident. Are you sure?"

Sage knew why she was asking, and felt compelled to lower her voice and say, "It's just if they change their mind. We don't have the funds..."

"You'll be taken care of," Micah told her firmly. He reached over and grabbed his bags, then said, "I can carry yours as well, I think."

"Nonsense," Mrs. Erics said. "We are quite sturdy."

Sage picked up her bag and offered a smile, hoping it might reassure him. "Yes, we are quite capable!"

"This way, this way please," a man called, and Sage glanced over at Micah.

"That's the engineer," he told her gently. "He is evacuating this car. You can tell he is an employee by the uniform, and you can trust him."

"Right," she said, nodding.

Sage followed the other passengers, and let herself be lifted down by the engineer. She hadn't thought about it, but the steps must have belonged to the various stations they'd gone to. Once Mrs. Erics was next to her, Sage glanced around. "Where's Micah?"

"Mr—ah, Micah is waiting until everyone is off, miss. He'll be right along," the engineer said, as he assisted the next person.

A moment later, Micah appeared, his bags in hand, and gave them to the engineer, while he jumped down. "Thank you," he said to the man, as he took his bags.

"We'll just make a line," the conductor was calling, from where he stood about a hundred feet away. "Everyone together, now."

"Anyone hurt in the other cars?" Sage overheard Micah asking the engineer.

"Not a soul, sir. And your car was the last." The engineer rubbed at his face. "Once everyone is in the town, we will send a man on to the next station to warn them, in addition to a wire."

"Thank you," Micah said. Then he turned and smiled at Sage. "Shall we join the others?"

Sage and Mrs. Erics fell into the line. The passengers moved at a steady, though nearly silent, pace, following the railroad tracks. There wasn't much around, other than trees off in the distance. While the other passengers glanced about, some whispering, Sage didn't feel very much like talking, she had too many worries in her mind. Despite what Micah had said, about the railway covering all of their needs, she was quite worried.

When her eyes found Mrs. Erics, she could tell the same thought was going through her head. "Thank goodness we have more than we let on," Sage whispered. "But how long might it last in such a place?"

"I don't know, dear," Mrs. Erics answered, but then she said, "however, I do know that so far, we've been blessed to have the help we needed when we needed it. Let us continue to have faith."

Faith. A small word, but one that meant so much. Sage nodded, and tiredly continued. The afternoon sun beat down on them, and she felt quite weak. Though she'd always pretended that she was strong and capable without having much to sustain her body in the way of food, the fact was she'd been far more tired these last few weeks, and the single roll she'd had today, nibbling on it as slowly as she could to make it last, hadn't at all done much to help her.

They'd been so careful, she and Mrs. Erics, not to eat much, in case they needed it later. Sage knew they were right, as now they might have to make what scanty supplies they had stretch even longer. No matter what Micah said, or how he tried to assure her, she needed to be prepared for the unwelcome expenses.

"Almost there," Micah said, from where he walked next to her. Then he frowned. "Are you sure you are well? You don't look it. Let me take your bag."

"I'm fine," Sage whispered, though she felt anything but. She tried to give him a reassuring smile, but her vision started to blur. Sage stopped to put a hand to her head as it suddenly spun, and the last thing she remembered was Micah's shout and strong arms grabbing her.

Chapter 9

Micah had been more than a little worried about Sage as they'd walked. It was painfully obvious to him how frail she was in body, even if her spirit was strong. When she'd faltered, and her face had drained of the little color it had, he'd nearly thrown himself to catch her.

As his arms went around her, she felt too small. Too light. Anxiously, Micah lowered Sage to the grass. Several of the passengers had slowed, but Micah waved them on.

"Sage?" he said quietly.

"Poor dear, she's so weak," Mrs. Erics said, kneeling next to him.

"Was she hurt on the train?" Micah asked. "And didn't tell me?"

"I don't think so," the older woman said. "She...she has had very little to nourish her body these last few months."

"Few months?" Micah asked, doubtfully. Sage and Mrs. Erics each nibbling on a single roll today returned to his mind. "Only a few? She is, forgive me, but she is far too thin, and you look it as well."

"Things have been very difficult for us," Mrs. Erics said, not meeting his eyes. "For the last year, perhaps longer, we've struggled, but even more so the last few months. We've," her voice caught, "we've been managing on a scant meal a day, and water."

"I get the feeling there's a good deal more to your struggle," Micah said quietly, as he searched the woman's face. "I understand I'm a stranger, but if it might be helpful for me to know..."

"There's nothing you can do, sir, though we are so grateful for your assistance on our trip," Mrs. Erics said. She sighed softly as she brushed the hair from Sage's face. "I've been with Sage since the day she was born, and her mother passed. Her father took sick and died a few years ago.

"Everything was left to her older brother, with the stipulation that he care for her. Wasn't long after that he married a woman who wanted everything for herself. Her brother gave her a few hundred dollars, and told her she had to figure things out. Just over a year later, he told her he'd sold the house, and in a few months she'd need to leave. We—" her voice caught, "we tried, but there were no options, and little work.

"Even in our town, there was no help for us. At first, Sage and I were too embarrassed to ask for anything from the church. By the time we did, we were told that there was no help that could be given, that we needed to work, to rely upon faith to see us through." She stopped and shook her head. "There was no work, though. No matter how hard we looked. Our faith we have in abundance, though I fear it does wane at times.

"This, Sage being a mail-order bride, it's the only way that she might survive. I just pray it's to a good man. And, perhaps even one who will let us stay together. I'll work for my bread, I will. I just don't want to leave my girl. Sage is every bit my daughter as if she were blood."

There was a soft moan, and Sage stirred in Micah's arms, then her eyes flew open. As she struggled to sit, Micah helped her. His fingers were trembling, a combination of the story he'd just been told, and his worry over what to do. How he could help.

"I'm so embarrassed," Sage gasped, her hands going to her cheeks. "I don't know what happened."

A hand on his arm, and a pleading look from Mrs. Erics made Micah swallow back the words he'd been about to say that he knew just what had happened. Instead, he answered, "A bit of shock, no doubt. But you've two choices. The town is just ahead and either I can carry you or I can carry your bag."

Sage laughed softly. "My bag, then. Please. I don't want to make any more of a spectacle of myself than I already have. I feel sure I can walk."

He helped her to stand, reluctantly pulling his arms away once she had her balance and gave him a reassuring nod. Before she could change her mind, he quickly grabbed her bag and also that of Mrs. Erics. When the older woman started to protest, he raised his eyebrows, hoping that she'd understand this was the price if he were to keep the secret she'd told him, and that she must allow him to help her as much as he could for as long as he was there.

He might not be able to fix their situation, but while Sage and Mrs. Erics were in his care, since they were both passengers on his railway and also now his new friends, he planned to do all that he could to take care of them. He just hoped they'd let him. Micah had no intention of telling them that this was his railway. It might make things awkward, and also cause problems with other passengers. But help? As a friend, he could.

When Mrs. Erics allowed him to take her bag with a nod, he saw the gratitude, mixed with a hint of worry. He understood now, far more than the first time he'd seen them shaking their heads at the conductor and clutching their bags as they tried to board the train.

This might be all they had in the world, and it was understandable that they were concerned with what might happen to it. And to them. Sage's fear over the railway providing for them additionally made sense. If the women had not even been able to eat, they were so badly off that even their daily bread was something they'd had to skip more often than not. Combined with the robbery taking what little they had, they were in a terrible position, and completely dependent upon the railway's care.

Micah tried not to draw attention to the way he was forcing himself to breathe. It wasn't because of the extra weight of the bags. It was his upset. How could there have not been a soul to help Sage and Mrs. Erics back in their hometown? They might only be in his care for a few days, but he'd be sure to get them all they needed. Neither would want for food or anything else. He would see to it personally. What good was money, if he couldn't share it with those in need?

"Let me help, sir," the conductor said, jogging up as the town rose ahead, and Micah spotted the familiar outline. "I've got a room secured for these ladies at the hotel at your request. The passengers are split between the hotel and two boarding houses. A few were near their final destination, and will be traveling by wagon or stage this evening."

"Excellent," Micah said. "This way, ladies."

As they approached the hotel, the manager, a man Micah knew well, was waiting. "Ladies, just follow me," he said. "Mr—"

"Micah," Micah quickly said. "Just Micah."

The manager nodded, and said, "Your usual room is waiting, sir."

Micah thanked him, then said to Sage and Mrs. Erics, "Why don't you ladies freshen up and rest a little, and meet me here in an hour? We will dine together."

"Here?" Sage asked. "But our clothes..."

"Are quite suitable, madam," the manager of the hotel said. "After what you've just been through? We get a good number of travelers, so you will see all kinds here. We aren't as fussy as some."

That seemed to reassure her, and Sage and Mrs. Erics followed behind the manager, who carried their bags. Micah waited until they were gone and left for his own room. Once there, he dropped his bags in a corner of the room and went to wash in the basin.

The cool and clean water was welcome. It felt good to get the grime off of him, and Micah hoped that Sage felt the same. He was worried about her. Mrs. Erics as well, but there was just something about Sage...

Briefly, his mind flashed back to the promise he'd had his mother make, but then, Sage's quiet admission that she was a mail-order bride filled his head with worry. He'd forgotten. What if the man was no good? Didn't care for her? She didn't deserve that.

Micah couldn't help but feel shame as well. When his mother had first told him about the mail-order bride he was to get, he'd thought how any woman who did that might be a gold digger or else be a spinster. He hadn't even considered that some might have no choice. He wished, now more than ever, he didn't have a bride on the way, so that he could be the one to rescue Sage.

What would it be like, him telling her how he felt? Irrational though it was, as he hardly knew her, Micah knew deep within him that she was the right one for him. While he had no idea if she felt that way, he hoped she did.

The way her fingers had gently probed the bruise on his forehead, how her eyes had been so concerned, her soft voice filled with worry as she thought about him. Micah relished that. Though he'd never had much experience with women, he did have a lot of experience with people being nice to him simply because he was Mr. Walker. Sage...she wasn't like that. She didn't even know he owned the railway company, and had enough money to keep anyone in a comfortable lifestyle. Her actions, her speech, it was genuine. She liked him because he was Micah.

Something he wished more than anything he could be. Her Micah.

He closed his eyes for a brief moment, and then returned to washing. As terrible as the train accident was, he had much to be grateful for. No one was injured, but perhaps most important of all...he now had a few more days to spend with Sage.

He'd enjoy every second.

And try not to fall more in love with her than he was.

Chapter 10

"I wish I had something nicer to wear," Sage said, studying herself critically before the mirror in the hotel room.

"You look lovely," Mrs. Erics said, smoothing back a stray hair that had come untucked from Sage's hairpin. "Even more than this magnificent room!"

"It is wonderful, isn't it?" Sage agreed.

The hotel was quite large, and their room had two single beds in it, with bedspreads in a lovely lavender, with matching drapes, a vase, and a plush chair that sat at a small table. Sage had instantly felt relaxed and at peace, and realized just how much tension she'd been holding. There had been the travel, and then the robbery, then her fainting...

Then there had been her time in Micah's arms, the fluttery feelings in her stomach when she spoke with him or he looked at her. She'd experienced a great deal more in the last twenty-four hours than perhaps she ever had.

"What's also wonderful," Mrs. Erics said, letting out a sigh of pleasure, "is being washed properly. Plenty of clean water, a lovely bar of soap, and a fluffy towel each to dry off with."

"Yes, the train was quite sooty," Sage said. "I just hope we don't stick out in the restaurant with our old clothes."

"We won't," Mrs. Erics said firmly. "You heard the hotel manager."

"I just hope he was telling the truth," Sage fretted, "and not just trying to make us feel better."

"There's not a thing we can do either way," Mrs. Erics said, the closest to scolding she ever got. "I am quite sure that we will not be the only ones here in this situation. Are you ready to go, my dear?"

"Yes," Sage said, biting back the other questions and fears that swirled around her. Though Mrs. Erics had reminded her to have faith, it felt so distant right now.

Together, they walked down the long hallway, and then stepped into the lobby, where she was relieved to see Micah waiting. How quickly she'd grown to rely on him, she realized. Her focus latched onto him. Real, solid. Just what she needed in that moment. Something to remind her that she and Mrs. Erics weren't alone in a strange place.

"I've got a table waiting for us," he said, stepping forward and offering his arms to them. "Shall we?"

"My goodness, it's been so long since I've been to a restaurant," Mrs. Erics said as she took his arm and Sage reached for the other, trying to still her thumping heart and the butterflies in her stomach that took flight.

"What a lovely treat this will be, even if it was a horrible circumstance that brought us here," Mrs. Erics said.

"I agree, and I'm grateful no one was hurt," Micah said. He stopped before a table and held out the chair for Mrs. Erics, and then one for Sage.

"We are so grateful for your care, and looking out for us," Sage told Micah.

"It's my pleasure," he answered.

A waiter arrived offering a menu to each. Before Sage could even look at the prices—which Mrs. Erics had, judging by her sharp inhale—Micah said, "Remember. The railway is providing everything. Please don't get something based on price, but what you want."

"You say so," Sage whispered, "but—"

Just then, a man approached their table. Sage saw it was the conductor, still in uniform. "Sorry to bother you," he said, "I just wanted to give you all an update. The train will resume in a week. Until then, the railway will pay for your lodgings and your meals. We sent an update to your destination station, so that they will know. Please, order whatever you like. It's the least we can do as an apology."

Before the weight of relief could lift from her shoulders, the man had moved to another table, evidently another passenger, and was sharing the same information.

"I dislike burdening the railway with our expenses," Mrs. Erics said, "but this is a lovely little treat."

"That's the way to look at it," Micah agreed. "I'm sure, even though the robbery wasn't the train's fault, they'd rather the passengers know how important and valued they are, than quibble over a few dollars on expenses. Now, let's look over the menu."

In what felt like no time at all, they sat before plates with chicken and carrots and peas, with soft, fluffy biscuits. It had been so long since she'd had so much food before her, Sage was sure her stomach had shrunk, and she wouldn't be able to eat it all.

"Their portions are generous," Micah said, slathering butter on a biscuit. "I never finish it all myself, so they always wrap the rest for me to take back for a late-night snack."

"It is likely to be the case for us as well," Mrs. Erics said.

"After dinner, would you ladies like to join me for a stroll through the town?" Micah asked.

"That would be lovely," Sage said. "After sitting for a day on the train, even with short walking breaks, my legs are longing for a proper stretch."

"Sometimes, after I ride the train, I feel as if I'm still moving!" Micah joked.

The meal passed with light conversation, and Sage found herself slipping into that fantasy, the what if she were just an ordinary woman, having an ordinary meal with Micah. It would be far too easy to fall for a man such as him. It didn't matter she'd had little experience with men her age. The fact remained, in her heart, she knew there was something special about Micah, and she longed to spend more time with him.

A week, a long glorious week in this hotel, and with this food, and with Micah nearby, it was like a dream she'd never imagined, and Sage hoped she wouldn't wake up from it.

The waiter wrapped up their unfinished meals, along with portions of strawberry shortcake, and Mrs. Erics took them back to the room, then pleaded fatigue, but encouraged Sage to wander about.

"But I can't leave you!" Sage protested. "And, you are my chaperone as well. What would others think?"

Mrs. Erics set the leftover food down and turned to face her, holding up a hand.

"All things happen for a reason, even when we might never know why. However, I feel this strongly. Micah is a good man, and we can trust him with your welfare. Beyond that," she gently took Sage's hands, "you may never have another chance to be with a young man you choose, even for something so simple as a walk. I know I can trust you to behave, and I think we can trust him."

Sage's lip had trembled. Mrs. Erics was right on all accounts, even if she wished it weren't so. Wished that she had more time with Micah. The opportunity to be with him.

"Now, don't keep him waiting," her friend said kindly.

Sage nodded, and quickly hugged Mrs. Erics, who had given her a gift more precious than anyone else could understand, and hurried back to Micah.

When she got back to the lobby, Micah's face lit up. "Are you ready?"

"I am," Sage said.

"Where is Mrs. Erics?" he asked.

"She was tired," Sage answered softly. "But she suggested I come anyway. Is that...is that fine?"

"I like that suggestion," Micah answered her, his own voice low, and sending a shiver through Sage that she adored.

"Shall we?" Micah asked.

They walked together through the small town. Micah pointed out various shops—the bookshop being one that caught her eye most—and Sage found herself slipping back into her imagination, and the what-if thoughts that always came up around him.

"Look, a wishing star," Micah said, pointing to what indeed appeared to be the first star of the evening. "Let's make a wish," he said.

Sage tipped her head upward, closed her eyes, and wished with all her heart. When she opened her eyes, Micah had just opened his.

"What did you wish for?" he asked.

"You know I can't tell you, or it won't come true," Sage teased, though she knew the wish she'd made likely wouldn't come true anyway. "What did you wish for?"

He took her hand and squeezed it gently. "I can't say either," he told her, but the way he looked at her, and the heavy silence between them as they walked inside the hotel, and he took her to her room door, made Sage wonder if it had anything at all to do with her.

Chapter 11

It had been three days. Three wonderful days of enjoying meals with Sage, going for walks with Sage, getting to know Sage, and falling in love with Sage.

Which was bad. Very, very bad. Micah didn't know how he'd gotten to that point. He knew better. Sage was on her way to be married. He had a bride coming. And Micah had the feeling he was going to have to be honest with the woman once she arrived. He wasn't interested in her. Additionally, somehow, he was going to have to figure out a way to ask Sage if she'd consider him, instead.

As soon as he thought that, guilt washed over Micah. What if the woman who was on her way to him was also in need of a home, like Sage was? This was a terrible situation he found himself in.

Micah glanced at her as they walked along the street. After the evening meal, it had become a habit that they set out together, walking until the sky started to turn crimson and orange.

Should he ask? Would now be a good time? He had wanted to ask her a little more about her upcoming marriage. See who his competition was. If she was looking forward to the marriage. How he could help her. But, how did he approach such a sensitive and private topic? Would she even welcome those questions?

He also knew that even if Sage were to give him the answers to his questions, he didn't want to ruin the moments they had together by thinking about or discussing such a thing.

They slowed, and Sage studied the bookshop's window as she always did. The last rays of the sun seemed to form a spotlight on the books. He noticed she enjoyed looking through the window here, but she'd never wandered inside. Why not?

Micah had tried to tell himself to stop thinking about her and analyzing all she did, but how could he? She was in his every thought. Her lovely face, her sweet smile, the laugh that pleased his ears, her clever mind, and her thoughtful way of speaking. She was intelligent, and he enjoyed talking to her.

It had been a relief to him too, that after a few days of consistent meals, Sage and Mrs. Erics were looking better.

Sage had a bit more stamina, and her complexion had improved with more color in it.

"Would you like to go in?" Micah asked as he saw the briefest of flashes of longing cross Sage's face as she studied the shop beyond the window.

"I don't dare," Sage said with a small laugh. "But thank you. We can keep walking."

Micah had noticed she did that sometimes when she was sad. A little laugh. It made his heart hurt. "Why is that?" he asked. "If it is on my account, I assure you, it is not a hardship. I enjoy books myself."

She didn't say anything for a long moment. Micah wondered if she'd even answer when she finally said, "I love to read. Growing up, Papa had an enormous library. There was most everything you could imagine. Books on history, on science, like the skies and botany. He had literature and poetry, genealogy, and books on animals, other countries, and a good number of religious texts."

"It sounds wonderful," Micah said, not needing to fake his enthusiasm. "I bet you spent a good deal of time there."

"I did!" Sage smiled, a true, bright smile. "Papa had a large table with plush chairs before it in case you needed to have multiple books open to study, but the tall windows also had cushioned benches built into them. It was those reading nooks that I preferred."

"I can picture it perfectly," Micah said. "How wonderful it must be! You must miss it."

Her smile faded, though her eyes never left the books in the store. "I do. Jerry—that's my brother—sold off all the books. I don't own even one now. He wouldn't let me keep any of them."

He sucked in a breath. "What a terrible loss. That seems very cruel. I am so sorry."

"They are...they were, just things." Sage's head dipped, and he wondered if she was trying not to let him see her sadness.

"But they brought you pleasure and wisdom, and were a wonderful thing to enjoy," Micah told her. "While I can't replace them all, we could start to rebuild." He reached for the door of the bookstore.

"No." Sage put her hand on his arm to stop him. "I can't. I dislike the fact, but I have no financial means of my own. Were it not for the kindness of the man I'm to marry, I would be penniless. I was given funds for travel expenses, but Mrs. Erics and I have tried to use as little as possible so as not to squander it. It doesn't feel right to use someone else's money for my own enjoyment."

She dropped her head, and said so quietly, he could hardly hear her, "We've even tried not to use any for food. In case the man wants it repaid. He might."

The reminder of her and Mrs. Erics slowly taking bites of their solitary bread rolls came to mind, and Micah felt pain wash over him at the idea. She'd been so careful. How many other women would do that? But there was such a thing as being too careful. Too restrictive with one's needs.

"I'm sure whatever he sent you, he expected you to use for what you need," Micah said, knitting his brows together. "In particular food. Why else send it? It's quite common, I thought, to provide for expenses to a traveling bride."

"Is it? In truth, I don't know," Sage said, looking at him with her clear eyes. "I've...I've never done this before and don't quite know. Not what to do nor what to expect. I also don't know anyone else who has ever been in this position, so Mrs. Erics and I have had no one to ask. We are simply trying to do as we always have, and be conscientious."

"You are too sweet," Micah said. "Too kind. I hope whoever this man is will appreciate the treasure you are and spoil you." He tried to grin, to lighten the moment. It came out crooked.

She just laughed, with more sadness than joy, walked away a few steps, and Micah hurried to catch up with her.

The mood had grown heavy. Micah felt lost in his thoughts, and wondered if Sage felt the same. He hated how much she'd suffered, and though Sage hadn't complained, had just treated it all as a factual matter, he didn't like it. Not one bit.

They finished their stroll, and Micah took her back to the hotel.

"Thank you for the walk," Sage said.

"I enjoy them," Micah told her. "I'll see you at breakfast."

She smiled as her answer, reaching for her door. As they parted ways, Micah started to go back to his room, then stopped as an idea formed. He changed directions, heading back into the street.

After he paused to let a wagon have the right of way, Micah strode back to the bookshop, and swung open the door, glad to have made it before the store closed for the evening.

The delightful smell of leather and paper hit his nose, instantly making Micah feel at home. He'd always enjoyed a good book himself. At home, he had a small library and enjoyed adding to it. It wasn't as large as Sage's father's was, but perhaps one day it would be. He rather liked that idea.

"May I help you?" the shop owner asked, glancing up from the thick blue volume he was flipping through.

"I'm wanting to buy a few books," Micah said. "Though I don't know what yet. They are to be gifts. If it's all right with you, I will just browse."

"Of course. Let me know if you need help. There's no need to hurry," the man said, pushing up his spectacles and returning to the book he was reading.

Micah roamed the store, looking carefully at the selection. He had decided to gift Sage a book, and so that it didn't look improper, give Mrs. Erics one as well. He might even buy one for himself. The store had a good selection, and Micah had difficulty deciding what to get. There were a great number of subjects, as well as a delightful selection of novels and poetry. He wasn't sure what Sage might like, but it seemed to him that she enjoyed most anything, so he hoped his selections would be ones she'd enjoy.

After a time, he chose a Jules Verne book and another by Charles Dickens for their gifts. The books were popular, thick, and hopefully would provide hours of enjoyment.

While he knew Sage would have refused his gift had she been there, she wasn't, and Micah was determined to give the book to her. In fact, he would inscribe it. If he never saw her again, after they arrived at their final stop and were forced to part ways, then at least she'd have something to remember him by.

Micah had not given up the idea of talking to Sage and telling her how he felt. He admitted it. He was scared. Scared to tell her, scared to risk what they had now. It might not be much, but it was something he enjoyed.

He approached the bookseller, and whispered to himself, "If only I had a way with words like these men do."

Then what? A small voice asked in his head.

Then, I'd tell her how madly head over heels I feel about her.

Chapter 12

"I heard that section of track is almost repaired," Mrs. Erics said, from where she stood in front of the mirror in their hotel room, pulling back her long, graying hair. "I have to confess, I'll be a little sad to leave this town behind. I've enjoyed it."

"I have too," Sage agreed. "Though, at times I feel bad that here we are, being spoiled by the railway company."

"Hmm, I suspect they are more than happy to do a little spoiling," Mrs. Erics said dryly. "Even if the robbery wasn't their fault, I guess it doesn't make them look too good."

"You are right on that," Sage said. "Micah said the same. I wonder how he seems to know so much about the railway company! I just hope when we resume, nothing more will happen that's distressing."

"As do I," her friend said. She glanced at the clock on the wall and asked, "Should we go to the restaurant now to meet Micah?"

Micah. The name warmed her inside and out. Sage hoped she wasn't flushed. "Yes, I'm ready."

Carefully, she locked the hotel room door behind them, and they walked down the hallway. As he had been each mealtime, Micah was there, waiting for them. Also, as happened each time she saw him, Sage's pulse sped up slightly.

"You are a dear, looking after us each day," Mrs. Erics said, as she patted his arm. "You've no idea how grateful we are for you. The thanks we can give seems meager, indeed."

"It's my pleasure," Micah assured her. "And, my privilege. Your company makes this time here much more pleasant. For that, I am incredibly grateful. Shall we go in?"

Before much time had passed, they were seated with tea, pastries, ham, fried potatoes, and slices of tomatoes. The meal was as every other they'd had, delicious. And, the company was exceptional.

Micah was good at carrying a conversation. It was clear Mrs. Erics enjoyed his company as well. Sage knew they'd both miss him terribly when they parted ways. She wondered if she could be so bold as to hint she'd rather marry him. But that wouldn't be right. She'd agreed to marry Mr. Walker. Whoever he was.

With a small shudder, Sage couldn't help but picture him. An older man, perhaps stern. Exacting. No matter. Whatever he was, she'd have to make do. There was no other choice. She planned to beg, whatever it took, asking him to allow Mrs. Erics to stay with her.

"Ladies, I hope you won't think me bold, but I have something for you," Micah said, bursting into Sage's thoughts and blessedly, pulling her from the worries and sorrow that always filled her at the idea of Mr. Walker.

Micah produced the two packages she'd noticed him carrying earlier.

"What is this?" Sage asked, as he handed her one.

"A gift from me to you," he told her. "I know you've had a difficult trip, and I hoped in some small way this would make the remainder of it enjoyable, and perhaps pass faster for you. Plus," his voice lowered slightly, and Sage was astonished to see him flush slightly, "I hoped you'd remember me fondly when we part ways."

"You'll be remembered far more than that," Sage said softly. "But I don't need something to remember you by."

"I can't return them," Micah said, his lips curving upward and a teasing tone coming to his words. "I knew you might protest, so I inscribed them."

"My word!" Mrs. Erics said. "Aren't you a sneaky one!"

"I am," Micah said. "Go ahead, open them."

Sage carefully removed the paper wrapping the object. She couldn't help but linger. It had been so long since anyone other than Mrs. Erics had given her a gift. She would treasure this memory too.

As the paper fell away, Sage gasped, and tears sprang to her eyes. "A book!"

More than a book, really. The beautiful, deep blue cover with gold lettering, thick, crisp-smelling pages, and a story waiting to unfold for her.

"My word! One for me as well," Mrs. Erics said. "You are so incredibly thoughtful."

"I hope you'll enjoy them," Micah said.

"You've no idea," Mrs. Erics said. "We both enjoy a good book, and these look to be quite enjoyable! I am very fond of Dickens."

"You are too wonderful," Sage said, holding her book tightly to her chest. She didn't miss the pleased look on Micah's face, and how overjoyed Mrs. Erics was. "Thank you. I think this will especially help with my nerves when we get back on the train. While I'm sure nothing will happen, I admit, when our journey resumes, I'm going to be a little anxious."

"I will sit right near you," Micah promised. "I'll see you there safely, I promise."

"Sir? Have you a moment? The train's conductor wants to speak with you," the hotel manager said, coming forward.

"Yes, of course. Ladies, please excuse me," Micah said, rising and placing his linen napkin on the table.

Not for the first time, Sage wished that she'd met him before she'd sent away for the mail order agency's help. But that was foolish. There was no way she'd have been able to do that.

In the lobby, she could see two people talking with him, the conductor, who still wore his uniform, and a woman around Micah's age, decked out in finery. Her pale blue dress complemented her blonde ringlets and complexion. She was smiling, and touching Micah's arm. He nodded to her, and placed a hand overtop hers reassuringly. Sage felt jealousy course through her, though she knew she shouldn't. Perhaps Micah knew the woman. Perhaps they were related.

And, perhaps she was just a fool. What was she thinking? This pretending, this hoping, it didn't matter. She couldn't ever have someone like Micah. It didn't matter how nice he was being. It was only because he was a good person. Not because he'd ever be interested in her. A poor little church mouse, who wouldn't bring anything to a marriage? Who would want that?

Sage felt her grip on the book he'd given her, the tome she'd cherish for the rest of her days. She'd have to be happy with what she was getting. A chance. Survival. More time on this earth. Love wasn't important. Didn't matter. It couldn't. Maybe...maybe she'd get friendship.

The woman squeezed Micah's hands, and then turned to leave, giving him a last smile over her shoulder. Micah returned the smile, while a tear trailed down Sage's cheek. No matter how she tried to tell herself it didn't matter, it did.

Chapter 13

Mrs. Marshall waved once more as she walked away. Micah was relieved that she wasn't upset about the incident on the train, and was simply wanting to let him know she'd arranged for alternate transportation to get home quickly to her husband.

Thankfully, everyone had been understanding about the train robbery, and the fact they'd damaged the tracks ahead of time. Without a doubt, everyone was grateful that no lives had been lost. Crews had been working sunup to sundown repairing the section of track; about twenty-five feet more, and it would soon be done.

As Micah walked back toward the restaurant, he glimpsed Sage. She was looking through the window. Was that wistful expression she sometimes had on her face there? What did it mean? He was selfish enough to think how he wished she was thinking about him.

Micah could hardly stand it. He wanted to tell Sage he liked her—more than liked her—but he didn't want to complicate things. It would be so easy to do that, and then to have an awkward space between them, or worse. She might get upset, telling him he was inappropriate, that she was about to be married. It might not matter what Mrs. Erics had hinted at, that the marriage was of necessity, not of desire.

The scenarios played through Micah's head, and none of them were good. He couldn't let himself think about the one he hoped most for, which was Sage telling him that she felt something for him too.

With a sigh, he started to return to the table, when he saw Mrs. Erics headed toward him, her eyes locked firmly on his. Slightly surprised, he waited, and as she approached she whispered, "I'd like to talk to you."

Micah nodded.

They stepped a short distance away, back into the lobby but further into a corner. Mrs. Erics was twisting her hands and looked agitated. Micah instantly felt concerned.

"Has something happened?" he asked.

"No, nothing that we've not already known about," the woman said, "but I've not had a chance to speak to you, and the more I think about something, the stronger I feel I must."

Micah nodded, though he felt uncertain. Was the woman about to tell him to stay away from Sage? Should he lead off with assuring her he wouldn't interfere in their plans?

Before he could decide and speak, Mrs. Erics said, "I hate to ask. You've done so much for us. Far more than you need to. But might I prevail upon you for one more thing?"

"Of course. Anything. You have but to ask," Micah said instantly, feeling better about whatever it was she was going to say. "Anything for the two of you."

It wasn't a false promise. Oh, Micah would do anything for Sage, anything at all.

"It's just you know Sage is to be married," Mrs. Erics said, and resumed her squeezing of her hands together.

Micah nodded, but was spared from forming congratulations or any other sort of thing he wasn't feeling when the woman continued.

"We know nothing about the man Sage is to marry. Not a thing."

"Nothing at all?" Micah's brows drew together. "That seems unusual. Aren't there usually letters exchanged?"

Though, he realized now, he supposed he knew very little about who he was to marry. Only what his mother had told him, and it wasn't much at all. For him, being a man and the woman coming into his home, perhaps it felt different. Less concerning. But for Sage and Mrs. Erics, he felt a surge of worry.

"Usually, and I think there might have been, had our situation not been so dire," Mrs. Erics said. "It would relieve some of my fears for her if we could stay in some sort of public lodging once we arrive. Just until we learn a little more about the man, you see. Make sure he's not one to treat my girl unkindly."

Mrs. Erics's voice wobbled slightly, as she added, "I've little hope I'll be allowed to stay with her, as a companion or a hired help, but at least if I know she'll be all right, I'll feel a little better when I am looking for work."

"Of course," Micah said. He reached over and squeezed her hands. "I understand your fears. You said he was from the town?"

"I believe so," Mrs. Erics said. "Sage has the letter. We were to meet him at the train station."

"How about this? I'll be sure to help you find a safe and comfortable place. I can't see the man would disagree, and I'll also look into him. Tell you all I know, and ask around if I don't know him."

Even if it might be one of the most difficult things he'd ever had to do. What if the man turned out to be everything Sage wanted? And more?

But then, of course, he might not be. He might be a man who spent more time with a bottle than anything else. A man who only wanted a wife to cook and clean. The kind of man who wouldn't love Sage, and be upfront about it. He didn't want that for her. In fact, the idea scared him.

But then...that might open the door for *him*. Micah's mind whirled furiously. He'd have to send a message to his mother. She'd promised, after all, to give her blessing and her help with his own bride, if he found someone else. Perhaps he could delay his own future wife a few days. After all, she was to be put into the hotel as well. And if things didn't work out for Sage... he could ask for her hand. He would make sure the other woman was looked after. Help her find a new husband. Explain he already had someone.

"I appreciate you so much," Mrs. Erics said. She glanced toward the restaurant. "We'd best return, so Sage doesn't suspect I spoke with you."

"You are right," he agreed, and joined her as they weaved through the tables back to their own.

Sage's head was bowed overtop her new book, and her eyes were wide as she read. Did she realize that she was near cradling the book, that one finger couldn't stop stroking the cover? Seeing the joy such a small thing brought her made Micah hope that even if he wasn't the man who she ended up with, she'd have someone who gave her all that she wanted.

Sage deserved nothing less. It was no use to pretend any longer that he didn't care or wouldn't let himself. There was no doubt in Micah's mind. He was in love.

Chapter 14

It was nearly midnight. Sage should have been tired, but she wasn't. Still, to be respectful of Mrs. Erics, she was holding as still as she dared, even though she longed to pace restlessly, watch the sleepy town through the window, drink some tea, or read. Something, anything to get her mind off of the person she was soon going to have to say goodbye to.

There was a soft hiss, and the room glowed warmly. Sage startled as she realized the small lamp in their room had been lit. "Mrs. Erics?"

"I sense you are having a hard time sleeping," the housekeeper said. "I am afraid I can't make us any tea, but I thought you might want to still talk?"

It had almost become a habit, on the most difficult of nights over the last year. Somehow, they found themselves both awake, both in the kitchen. More often than not they held cups with warm water rather than tea. Still, the heat had soothed. Would those days soon be at an end? Not because her worries fled, but because she'd also be separated from Mrs. Erics?

The thought brought tears to Sage's eyes, and she couldn't help but start to sniffle.

"There, there," Mrs. Erics said, rushing over to be at her side. The older woman wrapped her arm around Sage's shoulders and said, "Tell me what's got you so upset."

"Everything," Sage whispered, and her voice cracked on the single word.

"Everything?" Mrs. Erics asked as she sat beside her on the bed. Then she teased, "Even this delightful town?"

"In a way," Sage said. "I...I am scared. I find myself enjoying it here. The town, the hotel, the...the company."

"I take it you mean the company other than my own," her friend said, the teasing tone still in her voice.

"Yes." Sage lowered her head. "I can't help but keep thinking about what might have been, if things had been different."

"That is a dangerous game to play," her friend said with a sigh. "Oh, what I wouldn't give for a cup of mint tea just now. It always helps me think."

Sage leaned her head on her friend's shoulder. "I know I shouldn't wish for things I don't have. But when it comes to Micah, I can't help it."

"Perhaps I shouldn't have encouraged your friendship," Mrs. Erics said. "Something just felt right about it, though."

"I don't regret it nor this heartache at all," Sage said, sitting up quickly. "And I promise to do the right thing. To wed Mr. Walker."

"That's not what I'm worried about," Mrs. Erics said. "And we don't know marrying Mr. Walker will be the right thing. What if this young man asks you?"

"Why would he?" Sage asked. She laughed; dry, a little bitter. "What do I have a man like him would want? Why, even Mr. Walker will probably be disappointed when I arrive. I just pray he will let us stay together."

"Don't you worry about me and my future. But what do you mean you think he'll be disappointed? Why would you think that?" Mrs. Erics scolded.

"I don't know. Perhaps part of that's because I don't have high hopes, or any hopes at all, for him. We know nothing. That must mean there is nothing redeeming about the man."

"It's possible they simply left out the details in the letter. We will take a few days for you to meet him and get to know him," Mrs. Erics assured her. "Remember, that was our plan."

"I do," Sage sighed. "But it doesn't matter. I must marry him."

"We've talked about that too," Mrs. Erics reminded her. "Nothing is set in stone."

"What if he does turn out to be a good man?" Sage asked, sharing her new worry. "One I could like, but when he sees me in my worn dress and my old shoes, he won't want me at all."

"Then he'd be a fool," Mrs. Erics said with a snort. "Who wouldn't want a lovely young woman like you?"

"You say such things," Sage sighed, "but did you see that woman talking to Micah earlier? The way he smiled at her? She was so pretty. Dressed so well. It's obvious she lacked for nothing. Brought something good to a marriage."

"Is that what this is about?" Mrs. Erics asked. "You are feeling jealous?"

Sage ignored her. "All I could ever expect to have with as poor and sad of a figure as I am—"

"Now I won't hear you speak of yourself so! Why, you've got a backbone, more grit than most anyone I've ever met, and you've been through a lot as well. Now that you are able to eat properly, the color has returned to your cheeks. You might not see it, my dear, but I do, how Micah and others look at you as you walk past. They can't pull their eyes away. Any man would be fortunate to have you as his wife. Perhaps it will be this Mr. Walker, maybe it won't. But don't belittle yourself. I won't hear you do that."

"Thank you," Sage said softly. "I am so grateful for you. I didn't mean to upset you, though, with my worries, and

I hope I have not. It's all just so much right now, and we are so far from all we know. I hope we can stay together. I don't know what I'd do without you."

"Just fine, that's what you'd do," Mrs. Erics said. She sighed, and adjusted her sleep cap. "I hope we can stay together as well. But if we cannot, I will try not to go far. After all, I want to make sure my girl is well taken care of and has help nearby if she needs it."

A tired yawn escaped Sage, and all at once she felt exhausted. Like all of the stress had built to a point that suddenly overwhelmed her, and her body refused to think anymore, and only craved the escape of her own little bed, soft blankets, and a fluffy pillow.

"That's my girl," Mrs. Erics said, tucking Sage into bed just like she'd done when she was little. "Don't you worry about anything. It will all work out. You'll see."

That heartened her, but Sage couldn't help but feel like there were so many unknown things, and so much to worry over. Still the heaviness of sleep washed over her, and the last thing she remembered seeing as her eyes closed was Micah's face, his lips curved into a smile, his eyes shining brightly, and the night sky above them as he leaned in to kiss her, after whispering the words she longed to hear from him.

I love you.

Chapter 15

Just as Micah was readying to leave his room to join Sage for the evening meal, there was a knock on the door. He opened it, and stepped back slightly to allow the manager entry.

"I won't keep you, sir, just wanted to pass along this message that arrived."

"Thank you," Micah said, glancing down at the envelope. Slowly he closed his door, the weight of the letter feeling far heavier than he'd thought the paper could.

The message was from his mother. What did she have to say? He knew it would have been impossible for her to get the message he'd sent her last night. Reminding her of her promise, telling her he'd met a young woman he was interested in. He'd left out the part about her being promised to someone else; that part was best explained in person.

Forcing himself to open the letter, he scanned it quickly. Short and to the point, it simply said: *Train delayed. Miss Robinson arriving in three days.*

Well, that would be the same day that he and Sage arrived. There was only one train that day, so it must mean that at one of the stops along the way, Miss Robinson would be getting on.

Micah swallowed hard. Should he look for her? Let his fear build with each woman who entered the train? It would be difficult to see who entered or who left. After all, there were many cars on the train.

Or, should he spend his final moments with Sage as just that—potentially final moments? Micah knew the answer. He'd be with Sage. Not only had he promised her, he wished he was promised to her. He planned to memorize everything about her.

When he married Miss Robinson, if that's what happened, he'd be faithful, and his thoughts would only be of her. But until that day, he'd let himself love Sage, because a part of his heart, no matter how much time passed, would always belong to her.

A quick glance at the clock on the wall made Micah move quickly, and soon he was in the expansive lobby, waiting for Sage and Mrs. Erics. He saw her a moment later, but to his surprise, her companion wasn't with her.

Sage was in a different dress, still worn, but lovely. "That color complements you," he told her as she drew closer, and was rewarded by the pinking of her cheeks.

"Thank you," she said softly. "My father gave it to me the year before he passed. It is my favorite, and I've tried to use it sparingly to make it last."

The sorrow on her face made Micah swallow hard. He didn't quite know what to say to her. Hesitantly, he asked, "Will Mrs. Erics be along shortly?"

"Actually, as it's our last night, she wanted to pack," Sage said. "She is having her meal sent to her room and suggested we...that is..."

"I love that woman," Micah said, then realized he'd spoken aloud. He grinned, not caring if his cheeks burned, and offered his arm.

Sage took it, and did he imagine that she was closer to him than entirely necessary?

Their meal was wonderful, as each had been, but as this time it was simply the two of them, something felt different in the air.

As they waited for their desserts to arrive, a slice of chocolate cake for her and a wedge of strawberry pie for him, Micah said, "I know it's not my place. And it's not a topic I want to bring up. But I wanted to offer you something."

"What is that?" Sage asked, her eyes widening slightly.

Micah's heart started to pound. He wasn't sure why. The offer was in good faith, not because he wanted something from her, and he hoped she saw it for what it was. A gesture of friendship.

"When we arrive," he said quietly, "I know you are to...to be wed. But if you need anything, if the man isn't who you want to be with...if he...if something were to happen..." He stopped. He kept trailing off. It was the only way to keep from stammering, he felt so nervous.

"Micah, whatever it is, you don't need to be anxious when you tell me," Sage said in her sweet voice. "We are...friends."

"Yes, we are," Micah said, and hesitated, but rested his hand on the table. His breath caught as Sage did the same, and they each slid their fingers closer, a fraction of an inch at a time, until just the tips brushed.

Something about that fortified him, and Micah said firmly, "If you need help. If you need anything at all. If something goes wrong, I want you to contact me. I will give you my address tomorrow. Send word, and I will come help you right away. You have but to ask. I-I won't let you come to any harm, Sage."

The look she gave him, one of relief and anguish, would stay imprinted in Micah's mind forever, he was sure. A solitary tear rolled down her beautiful cheek, and Micah leaned forward to catch it.

"My love," he whispered, only belatedly realizing he'd said the words, "what is wrong?"

"It's simply that I wish I'd met you sooner," Sage whispered, her voice cracking slightly. "Oh, how I wish I'd met you sooner, Micah."

"I have an idea," he said. "Wait a moment? I promise, I'm not trying to end the conversation."

When she nodded, he jumped up from the table, and intercepted the server who was headed their way. A moment later, he returned to Sage and took her by the hand. "Come with me," he said.

She looked confused, but nodded and followed him through the restaurant and then out a side door. It opened into a garden, the one they'd visited several times. There, on a small table for two, the server had just placed their desserts and a fresh pot of tea. Seeing them, he smiled and gave a small nod of his head, then left.

"I hope you don't mind," Micah said. "This might be the last time we can be alone. And, well, selfishly, Sage, I wanted to be with you. No one else around."

"You make it difficult for me," Sage said, though she smiled at him.

"How so?" Micah asked.

"Because I am in love with you," she told him, her eyes honest, her expression open. "And I know when we arrive, I must make an honest effort with the man I am to wed."

"I've got to tell you something," Micah said, rubbing at his jaw. He sighed, not wanting to look her in her eyes.

"What?"

He didn't look up. He couldn't. Micah worried he'd kept this secret for so long that Sage would find him disgusting. But her hand found his, and he looked up, and every bit of guilt he felt likely shone on his face.

"My mother sent away for a wife for me," he told her. "In order to inherit my father's business, I must be wed by my birthday. I-I'd already planned to ask the woman to wait. I don't know who she is. But I could and would see her well compensated for her travel and help her to find a good man, one who…who isn't me. If…if you…if we could…if you'd…"

He sucked in a breath. "I'm sorry. You must think me a cad. I've kept this secret. But my heart wants you. No one else. You shame me with your sweetness and integrity. And I would do the same, I swear it. Make an honest effort with the woman. But I think what I'm trying to say is, if you need me, if you want me…if there's any chance at all, I am yours."

"I don't think you anything dreadful at all," Sage said, moving her chair close to his. "Nothing more than the man I love, and the one I wish I'd met sooner. You are just as honest, just as kind, and just as respectful as I've known you were from the moment I met you."

She rested her head on his shoulder. "I don't know what will happen, but I do know you will always have a special spot in my heart. Mrs. Erics says I need to have faith. This...this feels like one of those times that she'd say it, and so I must try to have faith that things will work out for both of us."

Micah turned so he could look into her eyes, and brought his hand to her cheek. His palm was warm, though a little rough. Time seemed to freeze, and Sage looked at him, her eyes flicking across his face.

What he wanted to say, wanted to ask...it wasn't right, was it? Micah didn't know. But he knew he'd likely never have another chance. If this was to be their only moment, dare he take it?

"Sage?" he asked.

She merely blinked, waiting.

Micah sucked in a deep breath. "May I...kiss you?"

Chapter 16

If there were the ground or carpet or anything else beneath her feet, Sage couldn't feel it. It was as if she were floating on a cloud as she headed back to her room. The entire evening had been wonderful.

After Micah had shyly asked to kiss her, and the world seemed to spin on its axis, he and Sage went for their usual walk, until the first star in the sky peeked its way out of the atmosphere.

They'd hardly talked, just taking the time to be. Something that Sage appreciated very much. She didn't want anything to ruin the moment, and was more than a little sad that their time here had come to an end.

When Micah had whispered goodnight, squeezing her hands gently, his eyes had spoken much more, and it was all that Sage could do not to suggest they be reckless. Run away.

She couldn't, though. Neither could Micah. They both knew it, and knew they'd do what they should. What they'd agreed to do. But that didn't make her feel less sad their time was coming to an end. Sage pushed that down, however, deeply aside. There would be plenty of time later to think on such things. But there would only be these final moments alone with Micah.

Sage turned the key in her hotel room door's lock and went inside. Mrs. Erics had already packed, and was in her nightdress, and reading the Dickens book that Micah had so thoughtfully gotten her.

Her friend looked up and asked, "Did you have a good evening?"

"The best," Sage told her on a sigh. "Too good."

Mrs. Erics didn't pry, just gave a smile that showed she understood, and said, "I'm so happy that you've had that." She yawned, and said, "Now that you are back, this tired woman will be heading to bed. Feel free to keep the lamp on if you'd like to read for a time. It won't bother me."

With a nod, Sage undressed and donned her own nightdress. A short time later, though Mrs. Erics had once again assured her she was fine, she'd blown out the lamp, and studied the night sky through the slit in the curtain. She should be tired, but she wasn't.

It was only natural that there was a good deal on her mind. Her time with Micah. The journey resuming tomorrow. Their kiss. What would happen once they arrived at the station. Some parts were so terrible, Sage didn't want to think about them. They'd come soon enough.

What was worse, she wondered? Having had the moments she'd enjoyed and experienced over the last few days, and then knowing she'd never have such wonderful ones again, or else going through life without having a moment of true love? Sage wasn't sure.

If the train hadn't been delayed, she'd have likely just said goodbye to Micah. They'd have parted friendly, but not as friends. She'd have joined her promised husband—hopefully with Mrs. Erics by her side—and started her new life.

This...this had been unexpected. And surely not what the Garden Belles had intended when they offered her a prospective husband! It filled Sage with guilt. She shouldn't have let herself fall for Micah. Shouldn't have let herself kiss him. She was a horrible person, the worst of women, and whatever her fate was to be, she'd deserve nothing less.

Her elated mood suddenly left her, and what had been, up until this moment, the happiest of her life, was now filled with the most crushing of guilt. The weight of it all was almost unbearable.

The only bright point was that, perhaps, there was a way out of this. Micah had offered, had even made her promise, that if she needed him, if she changed her mind about Mr. Walker, that he'd be there for her. In fact, he'd even mentioned to her he had his own mail-order bride on the way, and would provide for her as an apology for not choosing her.

It had been something of a shock, but when he'd further explained it was his mother who'd sent away, and how he'd known nothing of it until recently, she'd felt better. It was almost comical, how the two of them were being forced to marry, though for different circumstances.

Micah's promise to tell the other woman he was no longer interested played through her mind, making Sage wonder.

Could she do that to Mr. Walker? Could she dare to grasp at the happiness she was sure awaited if she chose Micah? Sage didn't think he was just saying that. Didn't think he was making a fool of her.

Sage almost laughed at the absurdity of it all. They each had a mail-order spouse arriving. She just hoped she wouldn't see his. What if she was beautiful, like the woman she'd seen in the hotel lobby? What if she was clever or well off? The kind of woman you caught your breath at and couldn't imagine being without? He'd never want her then!

"I wish I'd never started thinking," Sage muttered, flumping her pillow and trying to still her thoughts. The more she thought, the more her worries grew and the more difficult it would be to ease into sleep.

Sage tried to count to calm her mind. It didn't work. She started thinking of three and four syllable words, hoping that would distract her. Eventually, it did, but not until the sun had nearly come up.

Sage's bleary eyes felt dry and gritty. There would be no time for breakfast this morning, but the hotel was sending them with a bundle. She felt grateful for that. They could grab a small lunch from one of the sellers at a station, and then this evening...this evening she'd be meeting Mr. Walker.

Sage sucked in a breath, trying to push down all of her fear, and glanced around the room once more to be sure she'd left nothing behind.

"Do you have it all, my dear?" Mrs. Erics asked.

"I believe so," Sage said, with one last look. "I am a little sad to leave this lovely room, though. How comfortable and nice it's been for us."

"As am I," Mrs. Erics said, "but how wonderful we can resume our journey, and your adventure!"

"Yes," Sage said, smiling though she didn't feel the least like it.

There was a knock at their door, and when Mrs. Erics opened it, Micah stood there, looking as tired as she felt.

"Ladies, might I help with your bags?" he asked. "The train will be boarding shortly."

"Thank you," Mrs. Erics said, handing over her bag.

Sage did the same, her eyes locked on Micah's. He gave her a sad smile, and whispered, "I will forever be grateful for last night. Remember, if you need me..." He handed her a piece of paper that was neatly folded.

Without even opening it, Sage knew it was his address, as he'd promised, and slipped it inside her handbag. "Thank you," she said quietly, and then shut the door behind her, following Mrs. Erics down the hallway.

They climbed the small steps to the carriage they were assigned on the train. Sage felt anxious as the whistle blew and the train chugged ahead, lurching and picking up speed.

"Men are stationed all along the track," Micah said, leaning across so she and Mrs. Erics could hear him. "The track was checked this morning before the train departed. All is well."

That helped to relieve some of her fear, and Sage nodded, but she still felt tense.

The train's whistle sounded again, and the scenery flew past her. Once again, Sage was leaving a place she loved, only this one had been because of the man there. Her future felt so uncertain.

Sage gripped her handbag. Should she tell Mr. Walker she couldn't marry him? She had most of his money she could return. Sage glanced over at Micah. He was looking out the window, though the vacant expression on his face told her he wasn't seeing anything but lost in thoughts of his own, like she was.

She decided once they arrived, she'd speak with him. See if he was serious about choosing her. But first, she had to tell Mr. Walker she was sorry.

There was no way she could let herself love him, not when her heart belonged to Micah.

Chapter 17

The train ride was uneventful. That was good. Micah could see that it had relaxed Sage slightly, each station they passed without incident. She jumped off at one stop, but Mrs. Erics had stayed and urgently asked, "You promise to look into the man?"

He knew what she meant. And, he more than planned to look into the man. The idea of Sage being with someone who wouldn't cherish her and treat her the way she deserved hadn't left his mind since the moment he'd first learned about it.

"Yes." Micah hoped the short reply was reassuring. Sage was about to reenter the carriage. "Can you tell me his—"

"I'm back," Sage said breathlessly.

The color in her cheeks was an incredible contrast to how it had been when they first met. He was grateful all of the food over the last few days, and adequate rest, had erased most of the shadows that had been under her eyes, and had plumped her cheeks back out.

She smiled at him, and slid into her seat alongside Mrs. Erics, handing over the small bundle she'd bought. Micah let his gaze slide outside the window again. Another woman, around his age, was getting into the car before them. Was that the woman his mother had sent away for? He was glad that from the beginning he and his mother had planned to allow for time for them to get to know each other. He knew for a fact that there was no one who would be as suitable as Sage was.

The train pulled away, the station falling quickly behind them. The gentle swaying of the train could almost lull him into sleep, and likely would have since he was so tired except for one thing. He still didn't know the name of the man he needed to investigate. Perhaps when they arrived, he'd have a chance to see the man for himself and know instantly who he was. Still, not knowing was slightly irritating. Had Sage been gone just a moment longer, his curiosity would have been satisfied.

Micah let his mind roam over the other unmarried men in town. He couldn't think of too many. There was Jesse, a friend of his, and Tom, another friend. They lived in the town proper. As far as he knew, neither was seeking marriage. On the outskirts were a good number of farmers and ranchers, and likely one of them was the man who'd sent away for Sage.

He let his gaze wander over to Sage, and saw that she and Mrs. Erics had dozed off. Micah was tempted to walk through the carriage to the next car. Get a better look at the woman he'd seen. Even introduce himself, see if she was Miss Robinson. But he didn't. That would all come soon enough, and he shouldn't be in a hurry to be away from Sage.

Would it be useful to practice what he needed to say? So that when the time came he didn't trip all over himself? Micah frowned. How did one apologize proficiently enough to a woman who'd traveled expecting marriage, but didn't get it?

He knew that he wouldn't be the first man to choose someone else. Why, there were women who married on their way to an arranged marriage, and only stopped to let the man know. Or, didn't and simply wrote to them. So he shouldn't feel nervous. This was business, after all.

Micah thought carefully, then rehearsed the conversation in his mind.

How do you do?

No, too polite.

Madam, I'm afraid there's been a mistake.

Too formal!

Miss Robinson, I'm sorry. I don't know any other way to say this, but I'm not sure yet if I'm ready to marry.

Yes, that was a good start. Micah thought for a moment longer, and then nodded. Yes. He could start with that. Then, perhaps add on to it.

You see, it was my mother who sent away for you. Not me. As it so happens, there's a woman who already owns my heart. But, I want to make it up to you.

Micah nodded slowly. That didn't sound too bad. It wasn't perfect, and the woman might be upset, but perhaps he could make things up to her in a way more than she'd ever imagined. Hadn't his mother mentioned she'd fallen on hard times? He could help her find employment. Another husband. He could also tell her that he needed time to get to know her. Would that be better? He'd decided last night that no matter what, he couldn't marry right away.

Of course, there was still the matter of his father's will, and the terms in it, so Micah knew he had to marry. Maybe what he meant was that he couldn't marry anyone at all, until he learned Sage's fate. Then, he could either properly pursue her or else try to put her out of his mind once and for all.

"I never knew love could be this complicated," Micah whispered, letting his head fall against the railcar's window.

He let out a heavy sigh, and his mind turned again toward the man Sage was coming to marry. Who could it be? No one he knew had sent away for a mail-order bride.

At least, not that he was aware of. Micah stiffened. How terrible it would be if it was someone he knew. Like Jesse. There wasn't a woman around who wasn't drawn in by his baby blues and infectious laughter. Then of course, Tom was dark and tall and muscular. He had his fair share of women interested in him.

Micah stifled a groan. He wasn't any of those things that women found attractive. He was just himself. So, what chance did he stand if Sage were to be wed to one of his friends? Could he spend the rest of his days seeing her, but on the arm of another?

It was all he could do not to feel angry. Micah felt justified. His mother had interfered. He wouldn't tolerate it any longer. This was too much. Things had gone too far. Here, he'd found the woman he wanted. Instead of the obstacle of her traveling to meet a man—whom she could tell she was no longer interested in—they had that man and his intended traveling!

The train's whistle sounded. They were three stops away. The smoke from the train's funnel clouded over his window for a moment. Micah thought it was perfect timing. There was practically smoke coming out of his ears he was so upset.

Sage stirred, and the motion from the corner of his eye caught his attention, and he softened instantly. As she blinked awake slowly, he reached over a hand to reassure her.

"We aren't there yet. Three more stops, so about an hour."

Though she nodded, Micah didn't miss the way her face fell, how her hand clung to his, and how her eyes locked onto his own.

An hour. That might be all they had left together.

Chapter 18

When Micah told her they were almost at their station, Sage felt a wave of nausea wash over her. Mrs. Erics seemed to sense it and reached for her hand. "This is so silly," Sage said, with her nervous laugh. "I shouldn't be so apprehensive. After all, this is to be a good thing, isn't it?"

"Yes, and everything will work out. We must have faith," Mrs. Erics said, and then she bit her lip. "Oh dear."

"What is it?" Sage asked. "Did you leave something behind?"

"No, no, nothing like that," her friend assured her. "I'd meant to speak with Micah for a moment before we arrived. But, once we are there will do, I'm sure."

Sage gave her a curious look. "Speak with him about what?" she asked. Or, rather, she'd tried to. The train was slowing, and the loud whistle drowned out her voice.

“Do you know,” Mrs. Erics said, “while I’ll be glad to be back on the ground, I might just miss the lovely sound of this whistle. Isn’t it glorious?”

“Yes,” Sage said. “I never thought that I’d think so. Do you remember at first how startling it was?”

“I do!” Mrs. Erics said with a chuckle. “But the travel is quite expedient and it’s, generally, relaxing. Especially when you have good company, and a good book.”

“I couldn’t agree more,” Sage said. She let her fingers glide across the Jules Verne novel Micah had given her. “It’s been quite a trip,” she said quietly.

“I think I’ve seen more in the last few days than I have my whole life,” Mrs. Erics mused.

“It feels for me as though I’ve lived more in our short time away from home than I have the entirety of my years,” Sage said, knitting her brows together. “It feels so strange. I don’t think I’m the same person I was when we left.”

“Nor am I,” Mrs. Erics said. “And I feel like I can say that, even at my age. It will be an adventure starting over fresh.”

“Perhaps there’s someone waiting here for you as well,” Sage said softly. “Just in case we can’t stay together.”

“Well, fancy that!” Mrs. Erics said. “The idea hadn’t come to me, but maybe so.”

It had been a short stop, and the train pulled away again. One more stop, and then the next was theirs. They’d stand for the last time on this train, grab their bags, and step off the car and onto the platform. What would be waiting?

Her future husband, obviously. But what if he didn't show up? Such things happened. What if he'd decided against their marriage? Come to his senses about marrying a stranger? What would she do then? It wouldn't be right to keep the money he'd sent her.

"I can see you fretting," Mrs. Erics said gently. "There's no good in borrowing trouble, Sage. The Good Lord sends us enough to help us rise up and meet those challenges head on to grow. While He won't send more than we can bear, I don't want to tempt things by adding more to my load."

"You are right," Sage said, shaking her head. "I'm sorry. It's just so terribly hard."

"Many things in life are," Mrs. Erics replied with a sigh. "But we've gotten through them. We will get through this as well. Now, chin up, shoulders back, and let's look about this with the eye of travelers who are embarking upon a new world! Why, I'll bet your brother and his wife have never traveled this much!"

"Nor stayed in such a wonderful hotel!" Sage said. "Those desserts!"

"I am quite fond of puddings now," Mrs. Erics agreed. "Covered in whipped cream!"

Sage giggled, but then the train began to slow for the final time. In panic, she gripped her friend's hand. "This is it," she said.

Micah leaned over. "This is our stop," he told her.

She nodded. Though her heart was pounding, and her stomach rolling, and every bit of her felt as tightly wound up as a coiled rope, she tried to meet his eyes.

What Sage saw there was something that mirrored how she felt. "Micah," she whispered, or maybe she didn't. Maybe her lips only moved. The train whistle blew, and whatever Micah was going to say was lost. She saw his lips move, but was she wrong? Had he just said he loved her?

The brakes squealed to a stop, and Mrs. Erics set her bag on her lap. Her expression was grim, despite her talk to Sage about embracing adventure and having faith. Sage knew the words had been for her friend, as much as they'd been for her. Both of them were apprehensive about what the future held.

One thing Sage knew, however, was there was only the slimmest chance Micah would be in it, and they might not even get a proper goodbye. He must have known that as well. As the passengers stood, Mrs. Erics taking the lead, Sage felt a hand briefly on her arm and looked over to see Micah.

She couldn't do it. Couldn't look at him, without crying, without wrapping her arms around him and telling him she didn't want to leave. Micah looked as though he wanted to say something, but wasn't sure what.

Just then, the passengers began to disembark, and Sage drew in a deep breath. She squared her shoulders, raised her chin, and willed her nerves to settle. Her feet moved of their own accord to the front where the conductor reached for her hand to help her.

As Sage stepped off the railway car and onto the station platform, the past left her, and she chose to embrace the future, whatever it might be.

After all, there was little more she could do.

Pressing one hand into her stomach, and taking a final deep breath, Sage strode toward Mrs. Erics, who was waiting a few steps away, and then she turned back, bag in hand, ready to meet her destiny head-on. It was time to meet Mr. Walker, and see just what kind of a man he was.

Chapter 19

Micah followed as Sage stepped off the train. Before he could walk to her, a young boy rushed over. "Message for you, Micah, sir!"

He accepted it, gave Tommy, the stationmaster's son, a few coins, and looked at the front of the message. There was no mistaking it. That was his mother's handwriting. Before he could read it, however, he needed to let Mrs. Erics know he hadn't forgotten. And, if possible, he needed the name of the man Sage was potentially marrying.

He took a few steps toward her, when the stationmaster touched his arm. "Are you well, sir? We all have been worried, after news of the robbery."

Tommy stood at his father's elbow, eyes wide. "They take anything from you, Mr. Walker, sir?"

"Not too much," Micah assured the boy. "Nothing important or valuable." He addressed the stationmaster, "It could have been far worse, as you know. At least those men had some decency to slow the train, instead of killing us all and looting our bodies."

The stationmaster pulled off his cap and wiped at his forehead. "You've got that right. Just in, though, wanted to tell you, sir. The lot of them's been caught!"

"Is that so?" Micah asked in surprise. "That doesn't happen often."

"That's right," the stationmaster said. "Unfortunately, the items they stole were not recovered, not yet anyway, but at least those men won't be hurting your rail line or passengers again."

"Good news indeed," Micah murmured. He glanced around. "If you'll excuse me, I'm waiting for someone. Let me see if I can find her."

"She's over there," Tommy said, pointing to the other side of the tracks. The train stood between them, and Micah strained to see through the windows.

"You saw her? What's she look like?" Micah asked, unable to help himself.

The stationmaster walked away to help a passenger, and Tommy shrugged. "I dunno. Old. Short. Wearing purple."

Micah swallowed hard and nodded. Old, short, and wearing purple. That didn't bode well. It also didn't sound anything like he'd been led to believe. He let out a sigh, and turned to where he'd last seen Sage and Mrs. Erics.

They were gone.

He hurried along the platform. How would it look to call out her name? Terrible, that's how. But he needed to find her. Micah had promised Mrs. Erics to learn all he could. And if Sage was already gone...

Tommy passed by, a stack of newspapers that he sold to passengers in his arms. Micah called out to him, and the boy turned. "Paper, sir?"

Micah dug in his pocket and handed the boy more coins, taking a paper. "I'm looking for two women. One in a light blue dress and a straw hat, and her companion is much older but also wearing blue."

A frown filled Tommy's face, and he scrunched his nose and shook his head. "Sorry, Mr. Walker. Don't think I saw them. But I wasn't really paying attention."

"That's all right," Micah said. "Thanks anyway. Let me know if you see them, though, okay?"

Tommy nodded, and wandered along the station tracks. "Newspaper? Anyone need a paper?"

It would only be a moment before the train loaded its passengers and left. Micah studied the crowded station. Then he remembered the message from his mother. He tore it open and quickly read it.

I got your message. Wait for me at the station.

Micah glanced around. Was she here? He walked along the platform, now looking for his mother, the older woman in purple, Sage, or Mrs. Erics. He'd just gotten to the far end when he saw Tommy running toward him, waving the arm that didn't have the newspapers frantically.

"I see 'em!" the boy sounded. "The two ladies you wanted!"

Putting speed in his step, Micah rushed toward the boy. "You do? Where?"

"Over there," Tommy said, pointing to the opposite side of the train. "They're talking to the lady in purple I was telling you about."

Micah felt sick. What was the conversation like right now? He had to get to them. Had to reassure Mrs. Erics he'd not forgotten her request. Had to find his mother, and ensure she'd not forgotten her promise. Had to explain to the woman in purple that he wasn't interested in marriage yet. Had to tell Sage—so many had-tos.

"All aboard!" the conductor called, and a last-minute flurry of activity ensued.

Micah waited impatiently as the final passengers boarded, the train sounded its long whistle, and it slowly started to chug away from the station.

Through the cracks of the train, he could spy Sage gripping her bag, her face pale. Mrs. Erics looked pleasant enough, though by now he thought he could detect a hint of tension in her. And, just as Tommy had said, a woman all in purple stood talking to them, though her back was to him and her hat covered what little he could see of her head.

The last car rattled past, and Micah hurried to cross the tracks and get to the women. And whatever the future might hold, good or bad.

Chapter 20

Sage had never been so nervous in her life. She was so grateful Mrs. Erics was there. But how long could she stay? Worriedly, she smoothed her dress, then smoothed it again. Sage gripped her bag tightly as she glanced around the station.

"Do you see any men who appear to be looking for someone?" she asked.

"Only Micah, who was given a note and now seems to be trying to find the person," Mrs. Erics said, as she peered about herself.

"It's a little hard to see with so many people around," Sage admitted. "It's even worse when you don't quite know who you are looking for."

"Miss Robinson?"

Sage spun around, her heart thumping rapidly. Was this her husband-to-be?

A man in a railway uniform gave her a small bow. "There is someone looking for you. If you'll follow me?"

She swallowed hard and nodded. "Thank you."

"I'll be coming too," Mrs. Erics said, in a polite tone but one that brooked no argument. "I'm her chaperone."

"Indeed, madam," the man said, and led them onto a small platform and around the back of the train.

Sage glanced around nervously. They were opposite of the train station now, with the train between them and the platform. A woman stood waiting. She was about Mrs. Erics's age and size, and was dressed in a purple dress with a matching hat.

As they approached, she smiled warmly and held out her hands. "Miss Robinson?"

Nodding, Sage all but whispered, "Yes, ma'am."

"I'm Mrs. Walker," the woman explained. As Sage's eyes widened and she glanced at Mrs. Erics, the woman hastily added, "My son is your potential groom. However, I wanted to—"

The train whistle blew, and the words were lost. Sage wondered just how many times that had happened on their journey. It always seemed to occur at the most important moments!

"One moment," the woman shouted, and pointed at the train. She waved her handkerchief at it with a bright smile as it slowly chugged away.

As the train cleared, Sage saw a welcoming sight. Micah, rushing toward them, looking worried.

His eyes were locked on her, but as he stopped in front of them, surprise filled his face. "Mother?" he asked.

"Micah, darling. There you are. I was just speaking to Miss Robinson," her mother said.

Sage's breath came fast. She was sure she wasn't hearing correctly.

"Sage?" Micah whispered. "You...you are Miss Robinson?"

She nodded, her tone frozen. Thankfully, Mrs. Erics intervened.

"Do you mean to tell me, that you, Micah, are Mr. Walker? Sage's mail-order match?"

"I...I suppose I am," Micah answered, still looking in shock. He reached for Sage's hands, and she offered them willingly. "I mean, if that's quite fine with you?"

"Oh yes!" Sage said, and then the sob burst from her as she threw herself into his arms. "I'm so happy it's you! I'm so, so happy!"

Through her sniffles and her broad smile, and Mrs. Walker's surprised expression, Sage, Micah, and Mrs. Erics began to explain how they knew each other. Sage stepped back from Micah, though she still held his hand.

Mrs. Walker smiled at her warmly. "This is going splendidly," she said. "Far better than I'd hoped for. However, there's no need to rush. I've arranged for a room for the two of you at the hotel for a week."

"Then we've just under that to plan our wedding," Micah said softly. "If you'll marry me, Sage?"

"I will," Sage said, smiling so wide her cheeks ached. Then it fell, and she whispered, "But what of Mrs. Erics?"

"What of me?" the older woman scoffed. "I can take good care of myself. You'll see. I'm sure someone is hiring, and there's a lovely little boarding house somewhere."

"No," Micah said, shaking his head. "For the one who took care of the woman I love since her birth? You are family. We've a small house on our property, and it's yours if you want it. If you want a job to keep busy, then fine. But you'll want for nothing, regardless. I'll see to that."

"I-I-I don't know what to say," Mrs. Erics said, her face turning very red and tears forming. "That's too generous. How ever would you afford it?"

"Micah owns the railway," his mother said with a wave of her hand. "Or rather, he will own it fully once they are wed. Did you not know that? He has plenty to last a lifetime and then some. Do say yes, Hattie. I'd love to have a close friend nearby," Mrs. Walker said. "Do you like to travel by rail? None of my friends do, and I'd love a companion to join me. That is, if Sage doesn't mind sharing you. When Micah travels for work, perhaps we can all go! Make a lovely time of it."

"I don't mind at all," Sage said. "This is like a dream. I think..." She stopped speaking and pinched herself. The sharp sting faded, but she was still there. "And I think if it is one, I don't want to ever wake up," she said. She gestured to the train station. "You own all of that? Really?"

Micah took her bag from her hand, and placed it gently on the ground. "I do. I don't tell people usually. I want to be just Micah. Not Mr. Walker to them unless they work for me. And as for us, this isn't a dream, my darling. This is my wish on that star come true."

He pulled her into his arms, and Sage rested her head against his chest. "Mine as well," she said quietly.

Sage was aware that Mrs. Walker and Mrs. Erics had stepped a short distance away, chatting and giving them a moment together. She tipped her head upward and said again, "I'm so happy it's you."

"So am I," Micah said. He brought his face closer to hers, and said, "I love you, Sage. I always will."

As his lips gently found hers for the briefest of moments, Sage felt the world spin. A very different outcome than what she'd expected when she first got on the train, but one that felt perfect.

"Well then, let's get you settled into the hotel," Mrs. Walker said as she came back over. "The sooner we do, the sooner we ladies can get to know each other over some tea and cakes. After all, there's a wedding to plan, and my new daughter to make happy."

Micah grabbed the bags and led the way to the hotel. Off in the distance, Sage could hear the faint sound of the train whistle. The first time she'd heard it, it was taking her from all she knew. Now, it had led her here where she was meant to be.

Home.

Epilogue

"Let's see today's mail," Zinnia said, setting the thick stack on the table in the garden. "We've a lovely bunch today. Nine letters!"

"Goodness! So many. Shall we start at the top and work our way through?" Dahlia asked.

"Yes. I've the tea ready," her sister answered.

For the next hour, between bites of pound cake and sips of rose tea, they opened letters, made matches, and wrote letters to the future brides and grooms. Finally, they came to the bottom letter and Dahlia opened it. Something fell out, but she set it to the side.

"Listen to this!" she exclaimed. "It's not someone looking for a match, but someone we made one for!"

Dear Garden Belles. About six months ago, you matched me with a Miss Sage Robinson. I wanted to tell you how she exceeds all I could have hoped for in a wife. I love her dearly, and her companion has quickly become like another mother to me.

I can't ever thank you enough for your kindness, but I hoped to try somehow. Enclosed are two return trip train tickets allowing you to travel at any point to go anywhere you wish. There are no dates upon them, so you can travel as much or as little as you want.

"Well, isn't that wonderful?" Zinnia asked, picking up the tickets. "Perhaps we shall."

"Once again, a successful match," her sister said. "I cherish these letters."

"We do good work," Zinnia said.

"Indeed," Dahlia said, carefully putting the letter back in its envelope. "But speaking of work, the garden won't tend itself."

They cleared away their tea, put the letters where they kept them, safe and secure, and went out into the garden. The fragrance of irises, poppies, and sage filled the air, just like love filled the lives of those three women they'd helped not so long ago.

Zinnia looked over as there was a knock on their garden gate. "Forgive me, ladies," the postman said. "I forgot one of your letters."

"Thank you," she answered, taking it. Zinnia glanced over at her sister, slightly shaking the envelope. "I've a good feeling about this one," she said, and started to open it.

Want more?

You can find all of the Garden Belle stories here:

https://www.amazon.com/dp/B0CTHQJLKQ

Including two more of mine: Iris and Poppy.

***

Iris is a handful. Liam is in dire need of a wife. But is he *that* desperate?

Iris Green doesn't mean to be such a walking disaster. Trouble just seems to find her though, and scares off all would-be suitors in the process. Unbeknown to her, her mother submits her name for a mail-order bride, thinking that's the only way she'll ever see her daughter married off.

Liam Gardener thinks it's a hoot his potential bride has a flower as her name, it's a perfect match for his last name, so it must be a good sign. However, moments after meeting her, he's regretting it something awful. Iris comes in like a whirlwind and turns his quiet life upside down, and he's not sure if he likes that.

When two very different personalities clash, will the outcome blossom into something special or will their future wilt before it even starts?

***

She thought she was going to be a bride. He was expecting a governess. Will their misunderstanding end in a parting of ways or romance?

Orphaned Poppy Wilson is excited to become a mail-order bride. She's always wanted a family to love and dreams of traveling. Her match sounds perfect, and she's sure her future will be as well. However, the reality is far different from what she imagined.

Preston Parker is raising his nieces, twin terrors who are bigger handfuls than he could have ever predicted. When he sends away for a governess, he has no idea that he's accidentally contacted a mail-order bride service—and that his request for help was misunderstood.

Determined to persevere, Poppy agrees to stay until her replacement is found. Meanwhile, Preston tries to hide his growing attraction. Falling in love is a dangerous thing. Especially when his job puts everyone's lives at stake.

Note from Author

Thank you for taking the time to read *Sage.*

Could I ask for one small favor? Reviews like yours on Amazon mean so much to me and help others to find my books! Even just a single line means a lot!

Also...

Want a FREE book?

Stop by my website to get your no strings attached **FREE book**. It's my gift to you, as a thank you for reading this one.

www.sarahlambbooks.com

About the Author

Sarah writes captivating characters and clean romance that's anything BUT boring! From heartbreaking moments to heartwarming tales, get swept away in either historical or small town romance that pulls you in until the last page.

Nestled in the Blue Ridge Mountains of Virginia where she's married to her Texan husband, you'll find Sarah creating her next book, spending time with her children, or volunteering in her community.

Want more of Sarah's books? Find them all on Amazon!

https://www.amazon.com/stores/Sarah-Lamb/author/B098H3SGLK

www.ingramcontent.com/pod-product-compliance
Lightning Source LLC
La Vergne TN
LVHW090955080826
845145LV00003B/1014

* 9 7 8 1 9 6 0 4 1 8 6 6 1 *